At the age of 52, Angela Scholes, a married mother of two grown-up children, found a little time on her hands. A hairdresser by day who loved a read at night suddenly found a desire to write instead, leading to her first publication: *The Day I Fell In Love.*

To Lucy; what a good friend you were.

Angela Scholes

THE DAY I FELL IN LOVE

AUSTIN MACAULEY PUBLISHERS™

LONDON • CAMBRIDGE • NEW YORK • SHARJAH

A CIP catalogue record for this title is available from the British Library.

ISBN 9781528902038 (Paperback)
ISBN 9781528956628 (ePub e-book)

www.austinmacauley.com

First Published (2019)
Austin Macauley Publishers Ltd
25 Canada Square
Canary Wharf
London
E14 5LQ

I'd like to thank all my family, friends and clients for being both supportive and excited for me. To my husband, Graham, who never once doubted I could do it and especially to my dear old friend Lucy, who will never know that her treating us like family and being included by them to the very end would lead to my inspiration to write. Love to you all.

Marcos sat at his desk, head in his hands. He needed to go home, but home didn't feel like home anymore. And there were things that needed doing here at work. The problem was, though, to do things that needed doing, he needed to be able to think, especially as he was the head of a multi-million-pound company.

His phone was ringing and even before he answered it, Marcos knew it would be Katerina, his mother. Rightly so, she would be telling him it was time he was home, that she loved him, but he must face up to his responsibilities – something he already knew but didn't want to think about.

It seemed like only yesterday he'd had the perfect life. A successful business going from strength to strength and a beautiful wife, mother to their five-month-old son, Dante. But seemingly, he'd been blind to what was really going on around him. Something he clearly found out when he went home unexpectedly early one evening to spend some quality time with them and there was nobody there.

And when Alyssa did arrive home, she was in a foul mood, accusing him of never being there so why should she be expected to stay home. She said she'd liked her life better before they'd had a child and this life was not what she had wanted. It had gone from bad to worse. There had been no reasoning with her. Shouting at him that they weren't who they used to be, that he was never there and didn't care, she continued without a second thought that Marcos had no idea or concerns that they even had any problems. Finally, she'd picked up her handbag and headed out of the front door, shouting as she left, "You're not the only man in my life, Marcos, and how can you even be sure that Dante is yours?"

And there he was, left holding the baby, wondering if his son was even his or if her words were just angry words from a woman he'd thought he knew and loved. A woman who had clearly not taken to marriage and motherhood as well as he had allowed himself to believe.

Some hours later the doorbell had rung. He thought Alyssa had just forgotten her key in the madness of the moment, but it wasn't Alyssa standing there at the door. It was the police with the devastating news that Alyssa had died in a fatal car accident, and that now he really was left holding the baby.

The funeral had passed with many tears and condolences. Nobody asked the circumstances of why Alyssa had been out alone late that night. It had crossed Marcos' mind: *Did they already know and, if so, did they possibly even know more than he did?* And so Katerina, his mother, had come to stay, leaving her own home to be with him and Dante as soon as he had telephoned her with the devastating news.

Although now very happy in her second marriage, Katerina understood the true meaning of loss and despair, having lost Marco's father suddenly some years earlier. But she had trusted in time and love to help her rebuild a new life and assured him that eventually his pain would fade, and he too would want to build a new life and live again, that day was not something he himself could see, the pain and loss he had felt was not something he ever wanted to come close to feeling again.

And now, as if things weren't hard enough, his faithful secretary, who had been with him since he took over the company from his father and who had worked for his father before him, had fallen and broken her hip. Leaving him needing a temporary secretary as of yesterday.

The agency had sent him more than half a dozen already, and although they were all adequately qualified, he didn't feel he could tolerate one of them for more than three minutes, let alone three months. But his mother was right, it was time he was home; it was late and no good was going to come of any more time spent here at work today.

The house was quiet when he entered and there was a smell of warm bread and coffee coming invitingly from the kitchen.

"Hello at last," she smiled at him as he entered the kitchen. Now in her fifties, Katerina was still a beautiful woman. At only just over five feet tall, she was still slim, attractive and quick witted.

"I thought that as it's so late, some warm bread, olives, cold meat and cheese would be adequate. I've put the coffee pot on, but maybe you'd prefer a glass of red wine. Oh, and just in case you were wondering, he's asleep. That of course, would be your son I'm referring to." Marcos lowered his head, avoiding the watchful gaze of his mother as he felt the guilt run through his veins like water flowing downriver. He hadn't even given his son a thought, Alyssa's parting words seemingly leaving him devoid of all personal emotion. He'd heard them again and again in his head, so many times since that night.

"You're not the only man in my life, Marcos, so how can you be sure that Dante is even yours?"

He heard them clearer now and had done every day since the first time, her words echoing over and over again in his mind.

He was sure Dante was his son. Yet why then did he keep putting off having a DNA test? And now, when he spent time with him – which wasn't nearly as much as he should – did he feel himself holding back? He had never felt like that before that night. He'd felt so proud to have a son. The very idea that Dante may not be his would never have entered his head. But now he didn't know how he felt about anything anymore.

His mother's voice suddenly interrupted his thoughts. "Marcos, you should know I've decided to go home on Saturday. Pablo has hospital appointments coming up, and I need to be there."

Pablo was his mother's husband, a man he liked and respected very much. He was a good man, kind and gentle and from the very first time he had met him he had felt grateful

11

that his mother had been lucky enough to find love again he had made his mother very happy indeed.

"I could take Dante with me," she was saying, "and come back in a week or so, but I'm not going to. I love you very much, my son, as I'm sure you love yours. And although the circumstances are difficult you do need to face up to your responsibilities. It's Tuesday evening now so you've three days to sort yourself out. And now, I'm off to bed! Goodnight, my precious boy. The hurt won't last forever if you just learn to embrace the future."

And with that bombshell, his beautiful full-of-wisdom mother kissed his cheek and left him alone in the kitchen with his thoughts.

Morning couldn't come soon enough. Unable to sleep with a million mixed-up things going through his head, it was all Marcos could do not to go to the office in the middle of the night. But that would have achieved very little; he was already tired out and at least while he lay in bed, his body was resting even if his mind was running a marathon.

Making coffee later – a previously unheard-of task when he was at work – it made him think how much he had come to rely on others without so much as a single thought. Switching his computer on, he gazed out of the office window and couldn't help but notice what a beautiful day it promised to be. The sky was already clear and blue, and it was still only 6:00 am, but he was raring to get on with the day.

And though the agencies wouldn't open for another two hours, he was determined that by lunchtime he would have a secretary and a nanny. He had just three days to get organised, and this was day one. As lunchtime came around, he felt he was doing well, having found himself a secretary. Eleanor was a woman in her fifties who he'd met briefly before on a couple of occasions. She only wanted temporary work so that between jobs she could spend time with her recently retired husband. Fortunately for Marcos, Eleanor herself wasn't quite ready for that step yet.

The nanny was a different issue. Being too young, too old, inexperienced, over-stern – there really was no pleasing him.

Maybe tomorrow would be a different story, he thought. And hopefully he could find one that could start straight away.

At least Eleanor understood how desperate Marcos was and she was able to start work the very next day. But the quest for a nanny continued into Friday, with Katerina still saying she was leaving for home on Saturday. And by mid-afternoon, Marcos was despairing and even Katerina herself had also exhausted the employment agencies that dealt with nannies.

Marcos looked up from his desk as he heard the gentle knock at the door, and Eleanor entered.

"What can I help you with Eleanor?" Marcos asked as the well-dressed, well-spoken woman approached his desk. He already liked her. Her references were glowing and although she had been a real asset to previous companies who would have and had offered her permanent positions, she no longer wanted any long-term contracts. She was efficient, smart and understood the job and the pressure he worked under, and was direct enough to make the odd, quick remark to remind him she knew he was human as well.

"Your nanny problem, Marcos. This is just a thought – and I haven't even mentioned it to Lucy yet."

"Who's Lucy?" Marcos asked quickly, as Eleanor continued, "My daughter, or I should say, one of my daughters. She's just completed her master's degree in art and music and has been doing supply teaching at various schools. But it's the start of the summer holidays. She's moved back home with us while she looks for a place of her own, as she's applied for teaching posts in this area. I know she's a teacher, not a nanny, but she has siblings, cousins and friends with children. She's good with children and has time on her hands for the next few weeks so she might be of help until you get yourself sorted. Marcos could feel himself looking at Eleanor like she was speaking a foreign language. He wasn't denying that his bond with his son was poor, but this passing him from mother to grandmother to nanny, who wasn't even a real nanny, was getting very messy. "Anyway," continued Eleanor, "it was just a thought and Lucy may not even fancy the idea herself." And on that note, she turned and left his office.

At 5:30 pm, the lift door opened and out stepped a petite brunette of about five feet four inches tall. Maybe a size eight, wearing heels, skinny jeans and a floaty top, with mid length hair and stunning eyes. The internal office walls, made of glass, had always been a bonus for Marcos, allowing him to watch what went on. But today, it had just become more about the view.

"So, who was she? And why was she here?"

He watched her head straight over to Eleanor's desk and Marcos could see now that they knew each other very well.

So, this must be Lucy. Well, Lucy, thought Marcos, *maybe this is a matter I need to reconsider.*

Marcos, in desperation, had registered Dante for the best private nursery in the area, but he still needed a nanny – only now with a bit more flexibility. The nanny would need to be there when Dante woke, take care of him before and after nursery and until Marcos got home. And of course, she would need to be on call during the hours he was actually at nursery.

Marcos already had a housekeeper, but she just worked Monday to Friday, nine to five. This kept everything in order, yet still allowed him his own privacy. So, whoever took the job as nanny would have plenty of paid, free time, but would realistically need to live in during the week, as he felt it would be 5:00 am to 8:00 am and 5:00 pm to 10:00 pm at night, as well as being on call during the day, five days a week.

Curiosity had Marcos up from his desk and out of his office, and he was now standing in front of Eleanor's. She looked up smiling and said, "Oh, hello. Was there something you needed me to do before I leave for the day? Oh, and this is Lucy, my daughter. She's come to take me home."

Marcos knew he was staring at the two women, but it was the instant attraction he felt towards Lucy that had left him speechless. Finally coming to his senses, he held out his hand to Lucy and said how good it was to meet her. What he wasn't expecting was the electricity that passed between them as their hands touched. It was clear that both had felt it, and both quickly retracted their hands.

Quickly recovering, Marcos told Eleanor that yes everything was good for the day, he hoped they had a good weekend and said it was a pleasure to meet Lucy. But as he turned to go back to his office, he found himself turning back again and saying, "Eleanor, maybe you could run your idea past Lucy? Then let me know and we can go from there."

Lucy looked intrigued and glanced from Marcos to her mother, but Marcos simply turned now and went back into his office.

On Saturday afternoon, Marcos's mobile rang. Though it wasn't a number he recognised, he decided to answer it anyway.

"Hello, Marcos speaking."

The soft, feminine voice at the other end of the phone replied, "Hi, this is Lucy. I'm phoning to say that's the strangest job offer I've never applied for. But I'd like to hear more about it, whilst I have some spare time, providing of course that you are still considering me for it."

"Lucy, that would be great," Marcos could hear himself saying if a little more enthusiastically than he'd intended. He was also aware that the sound of her soft voice had stirred something deep and sexual inside him, taken him completely off guard like he'd never felt before in his entire life. And he actually felt a little guilty that after only one brief encounter, the electricity that had passed between them, was his reason for changing his mind about offering her the job. It was more about him than it was about Dante, his son.

"Can you come over now? Dante and I are both here. My mother has just left to go back to her home. I'll give you the address, or do you need me to come and pick you up?"

"Wow, OK and erm, no," replied Lucy whilst laughing silently to herself. "Just give me the address, and I'll be there shortly." And after doing just that, they both hung up.

Lucy arrived at the address about forty-five minutes later. Her poor, dilapidated, rickety old car looking rather out of place waiting at the grand iron gates for entrance to the long driveway leading up to the big house beyond. Well, she thought it may be old and rusty, but the poor old thing had served her well and was reliable, which was definitely more than she could say for some of the people who had passed through her life, including her ex-boyfriend. Maybe one day when she had a good job and better cash flow, she'd get a new one, but for now it was fine.

The electric gates began to open, allowing Lucy entrance into the grounds, she drove slowly down the long driveway, stopping a little way from the front door. By the time she had gotten out of her car, Marcos was stood waiting on the doorstep, holding the small boy.

Lucy locked the car door which she thought was probably not in the slightest bit necessary and suddenly felt butterflies appear in her stomach what a strange affect this man who she barely knew had on her she thought as she walked over towards the two of them. Noticing as she did how one looked full of mischief, whilst the other looked very tired. *The joys of parenthood,* thought Lucy. Not something she had a hankering for any time in the near future.

"Thank you for coming straight over," Marcos was saying as he welcomed her inside, her now following him through to the kitchen area where he was already making Dante some food. He explained it was his housekeeper Rose's day off. She didn't work weekends, so it was just the two of them home. In fact, it was definitely just the two of them as his mother had done exactly what she promised; packed her bags and gone home. Coffee Marcos asked proceeded to make them both some whilst helping Dante with spaghetti, fish fingers and alpha bites. Lucy could only watch, feeling a million questions springing to mind, but she decided it was best to let Marcos do the talking and once he had made the coffee, he said, "I'm going to tell it as it is, Lucy. Then, you can answer *yes* or *no* to taking the job."

"I'm thirty-four years old and a widower. My wife died in a car crash a year ago and until that day, I thought we were happily married. We were married for two years, following a whirlwind romance with only a few months of knowing each other. Alyssa was twenty-three when she died. I met her whilst out at a party. She loved life, particularly the high life. Dante wasn't planned, I was both shocked and delighted. Alyssa, though, was not so delighted. She actually hated being pregnant and didn't want to alter her lifestyle after he was born. I was busy at work and thought it was just hormonal; that she needed time to adjust. But that fateful night, I came home early and there was nobody home and when she finally did come home with Dante, she'd been drinking. We had a row because she had driven the car and it just went from bad to worse. She said she didn't love me and didn't want to be a mother. She had married me for the lifestyle, not love. So, my mother has been here for a year now, with her husband Pablo visiting. Sometimes they go home and take Dante with them for a week or two. My mother has been lucky enough to find love again since my father died, and as much I have appreciated their help, I knew this couldn't go on forever. They needed their own lives back and that's why I need you for Dante.

"I'm not looking for a girlfriend, friend, new wife or lover. I'm a busy man, who just needs child care for my son. I would need you to live in, as the hours are 5:00 am to 8:00 am in the morning. He can be dropped off at the nursery and then you'll be needed from 5:00 pm to 10:00 pm until I'm home. You'll also need to be on call in between, but off most weekends. Whether you chose to stay here, or go elsewhere when you're off, is entirely up to you but I'd appreciate you not bringing men back here, please. And your salary will be…"

Lucy could feel herself staring back at Marcos, flitting between feeling speechless and having the urge to knock his head off. She didn't think he had talked to her, it felt more like he had just talked *at* her. She could see the man was clearly full of guilt, but that wasn't her fault and she certainly wasn't used to being spoken to like that he was behaving very bullish – a mannerism she was not accustomed to or even liked. The brighter side to this, though, was that the child was so very cute. The wages were fabulous, and she could desperately do with more cash – and it didn't sound like she'd have to spend any time in his lordship's company. In fact, he'd probably send his orders via text or email.

"OK, Marcos, you got yourself child care," she said, "but I have to tell you I've applied for various positions and if I'm lucky enough to get one, then I'll need to start in September. That will give you less than two months, so you need to keep your options open."

Did I really just agree to this? thought Lucy, laughing to herself. She couldn't believe it. She must be mad moving in with a man she didn't know, even though it did sound like she'd hardly ever actually see him. She'd be looking after a one-year-old who hadn't a clue who she was, and she wasn't sure she was even that mad about children, so did she really want to spend that many hours with one?

But she had already said "yes" and she really had nothing better to be doing; it would certainly help with her money situation and she really needed to start thinking about a place of her own before starting work as a teacher.

All too soon she had been and collected some of her things and had now unpacked, had a tour of the house and been told to meet him in the kitchen when she was ready.

This, she thought laughing to herself, *could be turned into their conference room the way things were going.* Her bedroom she had been given was beautiful though, decorated in soft cream and powder pink, a winged, high backed chair in subtle beige check fabric sat in the bay window looking out over the walled garden. The walled garden was also beautiful, with many climbers in vibrant pinks and some honeysuckle growing up amongst the abundant flowering perennials and shrubs in the vast borders. The honeysuckle was a mass of blooms and even just standing there now, she knew that in the evening its perfume would fill her bedroom from the open window. The room was en-suite, with both bath and shower. Smiling to herself, she felt she may be very grateful for a long soak at the end of some days with a toddler.

Dante's room was next door to hers, and again very tastefully decorated in a soft, pale beige with light-blue accessories and white paintwork. It wasn't as big as her room, but it felt cosy and more comforting for a little person. It still had fitted wardrobes, his cot and a changing area but in his room, the chair was a rocking chair sitting by yet another large window which again had a great view of the garden. And although the two rooms were next door to each other, Marcos has given her a baby alarm so there would be no need to worry she wouldn't hear him if he needed her.

By now she thought it must definitely be time she made her way to what she thought of now as the 'conference room' – actually it was still the kitchen, but it was where she was sure she would receive her instructions. But as she entered, surprisingly the voice from the other side of the room simply asked, "Would you prefer coffee or wine?" And then Marcos continued to answer his own question by saying he thought it maybe should be wine now at this hour and asked if she was OK with a glass of white. "Sounds good to me," Lucy found herself replying and with that Marcos proceeded to pour two large glasses of chilled white wine, passing one over to her as she sat herself down at the large breakfast bar.

"I can't tell you what to do," he started, "but I'd rather on the days you look after Dante you have no or very little alcohol." He continued. Lucy was taken a little by surprise at such a comment and his need to say such a thing, granted he didn't really know that much about her yet but was he judging her on the behaviour of his late wife? She found herself looking, staring at him straight in the eye, assuring him she had remembered and understood their previous earlier conversation completely, when he'd told her about Alyssa.

And so she simply replied, "You don't need to ever have this conversation with me again – there won't be an issue I assure you." A moment's silence followed, both of them taking in what the other had said, before Marcos broke the quiet and said, "I'm making myself a bite to eat, would you care to join me? Or have you already eaten earlier?"

"Wow, so you can cook?" she asked with a raised eyebrow.

A smile crossed his mouth as he said, "I may not be Jamie Oliver, but I can find my way around the kitchen."

The awkwardness of the moment before now long gone, Lucy laughed and said, "Well, chef, if you think you can, I'll dare to take a risk."

And with that, he started to prepare a dish and topped up their glasses.

"Erm? I have a question, Marcos," said |Lucy.

"Questions – so soon," he grinned as he looked across at her.

"It's important," she said, already feeling the alcohol starting to take its effect. She'd been up early, eaten very little and was way out of her depth with this man.

"Who's in charge of Dante tonight?"

"Me, till 5:00 am," he replied. "Then you till 10:00 pm."

"Just checking before I drink any more wine," she laughed.

It had been a pleasant evening. In fact, it had been more than pleasant. It had been enjoyable. They'd talked, but it hadn't been about very much; just simple chatter and it had actually been fun. The drop-dead gorgeous, suited and serious businessman she'd first met seemed to still be at the office. And wearing casual chino shorts and a polo shirt, a funny guy with the same drop-dead gorgeous looks had been in the kitchen with her instead. It had actually made her feel like the luckiest girl in the neighbourhood.

Lucy could hear a terrible noise in her head. Her ears were ringing, and she just couldn't shut it out. Holy cow! Jumping up out of bed she realised she couldn't shut it out because it was a baby crying, the one she was being paid a ridiculous amount of money to take care of. Throwing myself through Dante's door, eyes half open, she collided straight into what felt like a brick wall, but this one spoke.

"Good morning, Lucy. Should we have discussed whether you are actually a morning person?"

"Good morning, Marcos. I'm going to ignore that remark" she replied "and I'll remember not to spend my nights off with you again! So, you can hand over the baby and go about your day."

It had been three weeks now since that first morning, yet she'd rarely set eyes on Marcos since. It was like being on the clock 5am Monday till 10pm Friday. Of course, she was off from 10:00 pm till 5:00 am, but by that time she was usually already in her room when she'd hear his car pull up. He didn't come and speak to her, so she didn't go looking for him either. It felt a little strange but not an issue. So far, she'd been as free as a bird in those hours when Dante was in nursery, she'd shopped, read, lunched, pottered, visited, but she'd become aware of a nagging underlying feeling – and it wouldn't go away. She realised she was starting to get attached already and as far as she'd seen, there had been no signs of her replacement. She and Marcos communicated by text as and when they needed to, yet they hadn't actually had a conversation since that first night.

'How's today been?
Is Dante well?
Are you OK?

Anything I need to know?'
And as usual, she'd reply:
'Fine.
Very...
Yes, thank you for asking.
No, but should there be, I'll let you know.'

'Well, today actually there is. It's Friday, and I've something to say and I need you to listen,' she wrote. *'So, meet me in the kitchen at 10:00 pm, with wine please.'*

And what was his big sodding reply?
'OK. X.'

Dante had been asleep since 8:00 pm. Marcos had been home since 8:30 pm, and Lucy had felt like an Alka Seltzer in a glass of warm water since she'd sent the text message earlier that day. Endlessly fizzing and unable to settle, she had to say it. She needed to ask him what was going on and tell him that this wasn't normal life. She was getting attached to his son and becoming the most prominent adult in his life, which she didn't think was fair to him. Where was her replacement? Was Marcos even really looking? She needed him to keep her in the picture.

The grandmother clock in the hallway was finally now striking 10:00 pm.

Hallelujah – wine time! Lucy headed down to the kitchen and there he was, pouring two large glasses of white wine. Looking up, he said, "I take it you're still OK with white."

"Thank you. Yes, that's lovely," she replied, all the while thinking: *Just pass the glass; any colour will do at the moment. The child is adorable. The father is unnervingly handsome and this all has to end soon before someone – probably me – gets hurt!*

"So Lucy...is there a problem?" he asked, standing there as cool as a cucumber while looking like a Greek god and looking at her as if she was some neurotic teenager. And she was looking at him, thinking: *Yes, there bloody is. I'm getting over attached to your son. I want you in my bed and I don't even know if I'll have a job next week.* But instead, she simply said, "No, everything is fine I just needed a progress report.

How's the search for a nanny going? Are you finding everything all right with me? And I wondered if you wanted to spend an hour or two with Dante in the week? You can, of course, take it out of my wages accordingly, but as I feel I'm bonding so easily with him, I don't want you to feel left out."

"Have you eaten?" was his only reply as she wondered which wall she should bang her head on. "No Marcos, I haven't but if you're worried about me having a glass of wine, firstly, I'm not on duty in the morning and secondly, there's enough of me to survive missing the odd meal.

"So, what's your preference Lucy – Chinese or Indian?"

"Chinese or Indian? She couldn't think!

"I don't know either. I take it it's been a long week then?" "Not at all," is all she could find to say as she just stood staring at him. What was it with him? His presence seemed to fog up her mind, his eyes seemed to smile as he watched her, and some form of little grin passed over his face as if he had just realised the effect he was having on her, then he carried on and made a decision for them both and forty-five minutes later, the pizza had arrived, and they had opened a second bottle of wine, although neither was sure that was quite ever in the plan, that is – if there was a plan in the first place!

Two thirds of a large pizza later, washed down with another glass of wine, Marcos questioned, "What's this really about, Lucy? What is it you're asking me?"

Lucy was tired now and a little emotional. The wine had gone to her head and the night wasn't supposed to be like this. This wasn't supposed to be life changing or everlasting, so why was she starting to feel like she didn't want it to end.

Suddenly she found herself saying, "I want to go to the zoo. I want to go to the seaside. All of us.

"I want to see you with ice cream on your shirt, to see you laugh, really laugh, for you to take the time to get to know your son. I mean really know him, not just feed him and see to his needs at weekends. I know you'll probably have a nanny soon, and I'll be gone, but you won't get this time back. You need to experience the moments and make the memories. They don't come around twice."

"I'll think about it, Lucy. And yes, I'm sure I'll have a nanny sorted out soon," was all he said.

So, that went well! she thought lying in bed, going through the evening step by step. *Chinese or Indian?*

So, we got pizza, a glass of white and two bottles later I still don't know if my job is ongoing? May as well have asked him if the cow really did jump over the moon!

Who knows? That question was probably on the same unanswered list for them both. Had she really agreed to this? She could have gone busking in the high street! She did after all have a degree in music.

Had she really been asleep? she wondered, as she rushed to Dante's room, the shrill sound of an inconsolable baby crying, sending her there like a bullet being fired from a gun. But Marcos was already there, holding a very upset little boy. And while her first instinct was to say: *Give him to me. I'll see to him,* it wasn't her place, so she stood back. But Dante had already seen her though and his little chubby arms were stretching out to her, leaving Marcos looking both uncomfortable and out of his depth, as he asked "Are you OK about this?" while having no choice really other than to pass Dante over to her. His little chubby arms quickly and tightly closing around her neck and the crying stopped, replaced with just little sobs as he soon calmed down, but the air was thick now and the tension very high. The silence between them broken only by Marcos apologising for disturbing her on what was in fact her day off.

"Just go and make some coffee please, Marcos. Neither of us wants to end up saying something we'll regret later." And on that note, she turned her attention to Dante, saying, "OK, little man, what's all this about? Hey, you're all hot and sweaty. You smell and you're not happy. Maybe those big back teeth are finally coming through, hey baby boy?" she whispered.

And with that, she took Dante off into her bedroom, thinking she may as well get the day started.

She stripped him off and cleaned his bottom and naked, they both slipped into the bath, where the warm water soothed them both. They soon started splashing and making bubbles, and she sang him a little song about fishes which soon had them both laughing.

"Your coffee is here," shouted Marcos from inside her bedroom.

"Great," she shouted back. "Thanks," and then followed it up with, "can you come in and get Dante, please, so then I can wash my hair."

"But…" he started to say before she continued with, "Just get the baby, please, Marcos. I'm sure you've seen far more before than you think you're about to, and I'm too tired to overthink this."

With that, Marcos stepped inside Lucy's bathroom, got Dante and left the room. Lucy washed her hair, drank the coffee, got dressed and then went in search of the men. When she found them, somehow, Marcos had managed to shower, and they were now both dressed, Dante chewing on a now soggy piece of toast. "Oh good, you're sorted," she found herself saying. "I'll leave you two to it then."

"Please don't," said Marcos, as she turned to leave the kitchen. "If you're free, we could put a quick picnic together and head off to the zoo for the day. Of course, I'll pay you extra." A slow smile spread across her face as she looked at him, slightly uncomfortable in his own skin at this point before she answered.

"I think the zoo is a great idea and with a picnic even better still. And yes, I'd love to join you, but don't ever offer to pay me for my company. If you want it, ask, and if I'm free and want to join you, I will."

Twenty minutes or so later, armed with their jackets and a picnic bag filled with all sorts of goodies, they were in the car and heading off on their way to the zoo.

It was a fabulous day out. And to the rest of the world, they must have looked like a normal family. They'd laughed and talked and enjoyed the picnic lunch. Dante had loved the monkeys and the penguins, and for the majority of the time, Marcos had even pushed the buggy himself and looked like he was enjoying the whole thing. The day had gone so fast and before any of them knew it, they were getting back in the car. Lucy, for one, wished it could have lasted longer. The journey home was very quiet, one sleepy baby looking totally exhausted in his travel seat. Whilst left alone with their own thoughts, neither Marcos nor Lucy seemed to have very much to say.

Once back at the house and with everyone inside, Marcos turned and thanked her for a lovely day, saying he hoped she had enjoyed it too and that they hadn't taken up too much of her time and that he hoped she would enjoy the rest of the weekend. Lucy couldn't help but feel like she had just been dismissed. Smiling sweetly, she said that she too had really enjoyed herself but then she had taken flight to her room, feeling totally crushed by his dismissal and struggling to fight back her tears.

After lying on the bed for an hour just listening, she could hear Marcos soothing a tired and whiny baby. He must have given Dante a quick tea, followed by a bath and now bed and she desperately wanted to go and take over or at least join in, but she felt she couldn't. It wasn't her place, and she knew she was already getting too involved. Instead, she grabbed her purse and jacket, shouted, "See you later," and went out.

So now she was in the car. Where did she think she was going? It was 8:00 pm on a Saturday evening and she was sure all of her old friends would be busy. She hadn't even made efforts to stay in touch with many of them – not properly anyway. She'd been away working and studying for a few years now. So, she decided to just go home. Mum was always glad to see her, and the house was always open to visitors. Being one of four children, it was rare if one of them wasn't calling in. And, she thought, there may be some post for her anyway. Though she did know Mum or Steffos would have called her if there had been.

Steffos was the lovely man who had made her mum very happy again Lucy and her family had come out here to Crete twelve years ago, because of her dad's job they had all fallen in love with the island, the lifestyle and the constant sunshine

– so different from the wet unpredictable English summers. It had been their idea of heaven on earth. Her dad had been a real family man, who loved his wife and children very much. But who also had a very good, but stressful and demanding, job in banking. And one day, he just came home from work, collapsed and died. Her family's world had been shattered. At first, her mum hadn't known what to do. There seemed no rhyme nor reason to her life. Everything was upside down. Should the family stay in Crete or should they all return to England. There in Crete had felt like home, but family was in England.

They were all teenagers, Lucy recalled, and it was considered a tricky age, so her mother decided it was better for them all to stay as everyone was already so settled. Her mum spoke Greek and English; she was a qualified PA and could easily find work. So the family had stayed, and it had all worked out well in the end.

And through her job a few years later, Eleanor had met Steffos. Like her, he was widowed, but not yet ready to give up on love. And that was what had happened. They had met and thinking that neither would probably ever love again, and yet had fallen for each other and had now been happily married for five years.

Steffos had taken early retirement and Mum was just doing agency work now, saying although she appreciated they wanted quality time together for holidays and hobbies, she wasn't quite ready yet to stay at home full time. She wasn't used to having free time, having had four children and a full-time job, whereas Steffos unfortunately had no children and although was used to a stressful and important job and busy life style, he had still been able to return home to peace and tranquillity. And deciding he was ready, he had embraced retirement and was thoroughly enjoying it.

And now as time had passed by, they had all left home, thought Lucy. Except Evie, who was engaged and busy planning and saving. Her brothers were married – Michael with a four-year-old daughter named Sophia and another baby on the way. And Carl and his wife, Maria, now expecting their first child. So, busy times ahead and good times for everyone.

But then there's me, thought Lucy – *and that was a different story.* University for art and music, a degree in both, then took up with a romantic loser, and now back home, looking for a job, because that kind of lifestyle was never going to last forever.

"Hey, Lucy," Steffos shouted as he came in through the kitchen door. "Are you missing us?"

"Like I would," she replied.

And at that he just laughed. "You want a drink? Tea, coffee, wine or a beer? How's life in the big house anyway?"

"It's OK," she said, "and coffee is great. Thank you."

"Your mum is upstairs. I'll give her a shout. You sure you OK?"

"Yes, thanks Steffos, and thanks for asking."

"OK, you just remember to look after yourself, you know we're always here for you."

Lucy's mum hearing her voice came downstairs, giving her daughter a hug before the three of them sat at the kitchen table, drinking coffee and chatting. Mum, as always, offering to make her something to eat as she did with all her grown-up children when they popped by. And although Lucy knew it was hours since she'd eaten, she had absolutely no appetite, her heart just wasn't in it. And finally, after finishing her coffee she decided it was time for her to leave.

It had been a couple of hours now and she felt ready to go back, so after exchanging hugs and kisses again and promising to come back again soon, she headed out of the door to her car, reassuring them once again that she was fine and that all was well. She'd only called as she had a little free time and wondered if there was any mail.

The big house looked all in darkness as she pulled up outside. After locking her car door, she quietly tiptoed across the gravel drive to the front door, slipping the key into the lock. Everything seemed so much louder in the still of the night, she thought trying desperately to be as quiet as possible.

"Shit, Marcos, what are you playing at, if you want to scare someone to death, at least wear a white sheet and look like a ghost if you're going to hang around your hall in the dark."

"Sorry, Lucy. I'd fallen asleep in the chair and heard your car on the gravel."

"Great! Next time reach for the light switch first, please."

"Sorry," he said again.

"It's fine," she replied.

"You OK?" he asked.

"Great, thanks. I've just been to see Mum and Steffos."

"Everything OK there? You seem a little tense," he went on. "Anything I should know about?"

"Would you care, Marcos?"

"Would you want me to care, Lucy?"

"Maybe that's the problem, Marcos. But thanks for asking and good night."

She was about to climb the stairs when one of his strong hands pulled her gently but firmly back and suddenly, they were face-to-face, eyes locked, hearts pounding and pulses racing. And a moment later his lips were on hers, it was like no other man had ever kissed her. And she couldn't help nor stop her arms as they wrapped themselves around his neck, her mind unable to decide if she was lost and he was saving her or felt like she was drowning. The kiss was so intoxicating she wasn't sure that if he had asked, if she would even remember her own name. Kissing her neck, then nibbling at her ear lobe and then back to her lips, tongues entwined deeper and deeper with so much underlying passion as they clung to each other, each secretly, desperately wanting more. Suddenly, breathless, Marcos pulled away and Lucy felt herself sway at the loss of his support. The passion of the kiss had turned her legs to jelly and her hands were trembling. Never had her body felt so alive and sensitive to a man's touch.

"Sorry, Lucy," he was saying, "I shouldn't have done that. I just don't know what came over me."

"Over us both," she replied, "so don't be."

And once again, she turned to head off up the stairs, when Marcos said, "Hey Lucy, it's not so late don't go. Come, have a drink with me." Now her sensible head was saying: *Just go to bed. This is getting dangerous.* But her fast working tongue ruled by her now awakened body said, "OK, why not? It's not like I've got work tomorrow."

And so she followed him back into the lounge. Thinking it was actually the first time she had taken a proper look around this room. And it was in fact beautiful with its soft cream walls, large sofas and a feature wall of warm-coloured slate.

Surrounding the large open fire lay a huge wooden plinth above and a marble hearth below. The cushions and throws on the large sofas were the colours of old gold and olive green with more colourful cushions randomly placed, Marrakesh in style in purple, gold and green with many sequins.

Candlesticks, picture frames and beautiful lamps added more taste and warmth to the room and a very large olive-green shimmering rug took pride of place in the middle of the floor. The room was both inviting and extremely tasteful, making it a perfect place to welcome guests. There had never been a reason for Lucy to come into this room. It was what she called a grownups room for entertaining family and friends, she had briefly seen it before on her first visit to the house. Her mind flashed back to her thoughts then of how beautiful she had thought it at the time. But when she was with Dante, her time was usually spent in the kitchen diner or the sunroom at the back of the house, where there were many of Dante's toys and the French doors opened into the garden, making it, she thought, her favourite space.

"Brandy?" Marcos asked.

"That would be lovely," she replied.

"So, you've been home to see your mum and Steffos tonight," he said whilst pouring her a rather large brandy from a beautiful cut glass decanter into a fine, delicate, large brandy glass, which he then passed to her.

"Yes, I thought I'd take the opportunity to go and spend an hour with them and check for any post."

"And you like Steffos?" Marcos asked.

"Yes, I do," she replied. "He's a fine man. He loves my mum very much, treats her well and has been a great stepdad. I hope they have many more years of happiness together. They deserve it, having both felt loss before," she said whilst sipping the brandy. It was very smooth, yet she could feel the heat and strength of the amber liquid as it slid down her throat. Leaving her not knowing whether she was a little tired, completely relaxed or just feeling a little heady from the alcohol, the ambience of the room and the presence of Marcos around her. What she did know was that she mustn't drink it too fast.

His eyes were watching her now. Sitting on opposite sofas she felt like a mouse being watched by a cat, anticipation hanging in the air

"And what about you, Lucy?" he asked. "What about your life? Your hopes and dreams."

"The answer to that is, I don't really know yet, Marcos," she said. "If I'm truthful, what I can tell you is that life got a bit messy and I'm trying to make a new plan."

She told him how she'd being studying for her master's in music and art and had now graduated, which was great. In between, she'd done supply work near where she'd lived and that had been fine. But Nikos, her partner, had been a romantic dreamer and that had also been fine in the early days. In fact, it was quite fun, him playing gigs and the two of them permanently partying, just drifting from day to day. But eventually, she realised that one day everyone needed to grow up – or at least she did. And suddenly, it just wasn't quite so much fun anymore. With the break up came the fact she was homeless and so she had come home to Mum and Steffos, temporarily of course.

"This will help me to save for a place of my own. And I've applied for some teaching posts locally, so we'll see what happens. I'm twenty-seven years old, Marcos, and I want so much more than what I've had."

"So, we might not get to keep you for long then," Marcos said, whist still watching Lucy, who seemed to be struggling for an answer.

"Who knows, Marcos? These things take time and you may also get sorted with a new nanny soon and be glad to get rid of me," she laughed, swallowing the last of her brandy. And with that she said, "I think it's time I went up. Thank you for the brandy and the chat, Marcos."

"You're welcome anytime, Lucy, and sorry about earlier, the kiss."

"Don't be, Marcos. I'm not."

The next morning, after she'd showered and gone downstairs, she found the house very quiet, and then realised that was in fact because it was empty. Feeling more than a little disappointed, she headed to the kitchen to make some coffee. And it was there, that she found the note which simply read:

'I've taken Dante to the park and gone to do a little shopping for supper. Thought you might enjoy a little free time in the house by yourself!

Treat it like your own and if you're free later and would like to join me, I'll cook you dinner M. X.'

Her disappointment had now just spiralled from disappointment to excitement. She felt like phoning him and saying, "Yes! Yes! Yes!" *But no,* she thought, *stay calm,* and so instead, she simply sent a text message in reply, saying:

'Thank you for your consideration. And no, I don't have any plans. So yes, you offering to cook dinner for me sounds good. Thank you. L. X.'

Sometime later, she heard his car pull up on the gravel drive and she couldn't help the feeling of butterflies in her stomach as she came down the stairs to meet them as they came through the front door. She knew she was smiling like the cat that had got the cream, but when she looked, so were they!

And once in the kitchen the chatter began. They'd had fun today, fed the ducks, been to the local café for lunch and picked up some food for the evening meal on the way back, together with a bunch of simple white flowers, which Marcos had now given to Dante, telling him to pass them to Lucy. At the same time he was asking her how her day had been. "Nothing quite as exciting as yours I'm afraid," she replied. "I've had a bath, painted my toe nails, read a magazine, sat in the garden in the sunshine." She left out the part where she'd spent most of the day thinking about them and wondering what they were doing.

"So, just a girly day. But you've done well. I must say I'm quite impressed.

"I didn't plan the day it just happened," said Marcos. "I wasn't looking forward to it really, but after your text my whole day ahead felt so much better."

She couldn't help but smile again at him and answered with, "So did mine, and I'm sure you enjoyed spending some quality time with Dante."

"I do love him, Lucy, but if I'm honest, I keep hearing Alyssa's words that he may not be mine, and I wonder if someone, some day is going to turn up and shatter my world."

"Then why not have a DNA test?" she asked.

"Because what if he's not mine and I know, and nobody challenges it. I'll keep wondering who his real father is and I'll need to tell him at some point. Then, he'll want to go and look for him when he's old enough. At least this way, I can believe he is mine," replied Marcos.

"You can, Marcos, but not knowing is holding the power and strength of your love back and that's not fair to either of you."

"Anyway," he said, "Let's talk about it tonight. What time do you want to eat? I thought I'd feed Dante and then get him settled before I start our meal."

"That's fine by me," she smiled, "would it help if after his tea, I bath and sort him out?"

"That would be a great idea if that's OK with you." And so, that's what they did. Dante had his tea, Lucy bathed him and got him dressed for bed, brought him down to say good night, then went back up, laying him in his cot so she could sing him some nursery rhymes. Whilst she stroked his forehead gently, brushing back his fringe with her fingers and holding his little chubby hand in hers.

He really was such a delightful baby and very soon he was fast asleep, looking beautiful and peaceful as only babies do.

Downstairs, she could hear Marcos in the kitchen. The food was cooking, and it smelled delicious. Lucy thought it was rather nice to think they were sharing dinner and better still, that Marcos was actually doing the cooking. It was also nice that Rose, the housekeeper, didn't work at weekends and although she was a lovely lady, Lucy found herself loving the freedom of it all, just being the three of them. She felt they were all actually getting to know one another.

"Here or the main dining room?" Marcos asked, as she entered the kitchen diner.

"Here please. It's far less formal, unlike the main dining room, and that's not what this is about."

"What is this about, Lucy?" he asked. And he gave her that look again, holding her still, not allowing any part of her to move.

"It's about you showing off your culinary skills," she said. "Marcos," she grinned at him wickedly, "be a good man and pour the wine, please. It all counts towards my five a day. And I'm off duty tomorrow," she said, as she gave him a little wink.

The food was delicious. The man could definitely hold his own in the kitchen. The starter was king prawns served in a mild chilli and lemon dressing on a bed of avocados, followed by sea food risotto and completing the meal, panna cotta served with fresh raspberry compote, all washed down with lots of talk, laughter and wine. What a lovely night they'd had! And all Lucy could think was she never wanted it to end, neither did she want him to find a nanny because she also didn't ever want to leave.

"Shall we have a coffee and a brandy in the lounge?" asked Marcos, bringing her thoughts back to the present moment.

"What about we clear up first?" she suggested, but he insisted he'd take care of that later or in the morning. So, they retired to the lounge with a tray holding a cafetiere of filter coffee and went to find the brandy. Sitting opposite each other on the big plush sofas, as if they weren't sure were each other should be, it didn't feel as comfortable and cosy as in the kitchen. The intimacy was lost in the vast space. It was of course a beautiful space, but it just wasn't quite like being sat at the breakfast bar, where it all felt so natural and easy. Now it felt almost formal and definitely a little awkward and Lucy could tell Marcos felt the same. They had lost the moment.

Maybe under the circumstances, that wasn't such a bad thing, she thought. She drank her coffee and brandy and got up off the sofa and decided it was time she said good night. Earlier, it had almost felt like they were heading for another kiss. But somehow the moment had been completely lost in the big room.

And so, off to bed she'd gone, thanking him for a lovely evening as she left the room to go and lie in bed to dream of things she dare not wish for.

When she woke, she couldn't believe she'd been asleep for less than three hours. Having come up to bed at around midnight, she had surprisingly drifted off rather quickly, but that must have been the wine and the brandy as it was now 3:00 am and she was wide awake, reliving the evening before. After twenty minutes or so of lying there, going over and over the same things, she'd had enough. *Why did he treat me so special, yet makes no definite move towards me,* she thought.

Deciding there was no point in lying there any longer, she thought she may as well get up and go and make a cup of tea. With her dressing gown on, she crept down the stairs and into the kitchen; the house was so quiet. *Bloody hell!* She didn't remember them leaving this much mess last night. *A good time certainly masked that one!* Well, she might as well get started – in no time at all the kettle was switched on, the hot water was running and the dishwasher door was open. *Easy. Here we go.* It had to be said, he may have been a fabulous cook, but she didn't think he had left anything in the kitchen unused. But twenty minutes later, she was doing well – pans washed, dishes loaded, tea in the cup and she was just wiping down. *Good. No problem!*

"What are you doing up?" a voice behind her said.

"Holy Hell, Marcos! Are you still practising that creeping around, because I can assure you, you're very good at it now, so you can give it up," Lucy exclaimed.

But he just stood smiling at her like it was a game and he was winning and Lucy was sure that any minute now, she was going to have a fit. "Make yourself useful," she said, "and finish making my tea whilst I wipe down and if you're going to hang around, make yourself one too."

"So, why are you up?" he asked.

"Probably for the same reason as you," she replied. "Couldn't sleep."

"Is there a reason for that?" he asked, staring straight at her.

"Maybe the same one as you," she replied. "So, what was it?"

Still staring intently at her, he said, "I'm not sure yet. I'm working hard on working it out. So, what are your plans for today, Lucy? Other than catching up on your sleep?"

"I'm not sure yet, Marcos, but I'm sure I'll find plenty to fill my time," she said.

"Spend the day with me? With us."

"You don't need to worry, Marcos. I'll be fine on my own, so go and have your fun. You don't need me to tag along."

"I'd like you to tag along. I'd like you to spend the day with us," he answered.

And so they did spend the day together – and the evening – and before they knew it, it was Monday again, and they were all back in the usual routine. Only the routine had changed each night after Dante had gone to bed and Marcos had come home. They had supper together and shared each other's day. There were times when it was almost too much – the attraction. And she could feel it equally in his body language.

The plus side was that it wasn't spoiling their working relationship and they were enjoying getting to know each other so well. It was amazing how comfortable they'd become in each other's company in such a short time.

Then one night, Marcos came home, and Lucy said, "Hello. I didn't hear you come in."

"I guessed that when I saw you a million miles away, care to share," he'd replied.

"Ha Ha! I was nowhere exciting. Are you getting changed before we eat? Shall I pour you a beer?"

"Sounds like a good idea and yes, in a minute. Have you got a drink? I want to ask you something."

"Fire away," she laughed, but curiosity had her and suddenly a little nervous waiting with bated breath.

"I have an important business dinner party I need to attend and I need a date. It would look so much better if I'm accompanied and it would stop any unwanted attention."

"Am I missing something here, Marcos?"

"I'm asking you, Lucy. Will you please be my date for the evening? I'll arrange a babysitter, or phone my mother, and I'll buy you a new dress and whatever else you would like for the occasion – shoes, hair, nails, jewellery, anything. It's a very big and important evening."

"Why Marcos? Why me?" she found herself asking. "There must be endless women out there who would want to be your date for the evening, who I'm sure would look stunning and play a far better role than I could, fitting into your world perfectly."

"I'm sure there are, Lucy. But you're the only date I want for the evening, and nobody could outshine you.

"Are you going to answer, or do you need time to think about it?"

"Are you sure, Marcos?"

"I'm very sure, Lucy."

She took a deep breath, excited to be asked, nervous about what it might entail and decided,

"OK, then you've got yourself a date, but on your head be it. I'm not in the same league as some of the other women I've seen when I've been to your office."

"No, Lucy. You're in a league of your own and that's what I like about you. Now, I'm going to change whilst you serve dinner. Just give me five minutes, please."

Five minutes later, Marcos returned to the kitchen wearing shorts and a T-shirt and nothing on his feet. *How does he manage to look so sexy in just about any look he wants, without even knowing it?* Lucy's head was still reeling from the earlier conversation. She was going to be seen as his date for the evening and although she knew it was not a real date, the thought of it filled her with both fear and excitement at the same time. She would be dressed in finery and be able to stay close to him all night – not as the babysitter, nor the child-minder who cooks dinner and stays for a chat.

It's a date even if it's not a real date.

"I think you're daydreaming again," he said, seating himself at the breakfast bar and breaking into her thoughts.

"Ha! Maybe just a little. And no, you can't ask what about! And anyway, when is this big event," she asked, unable to control a very excited smile.

"A week on Saturday. You still OK with that?"

"Yes, I'm fine," she answered, thinking: *Oh my God! So soon.*

"I've had a credit card done for you, so feel free to buy yourself an expensive evening dress and all that goes with it. And don't worry about the cost. The card is yours to use and has a ten thousand limit. So, I'm sure you'll be able to get everything you need for the evening, and then in the future, anything you think Dante should have. Or for the two of you to go places and of course for other purchases for other occasions that may arise, where maybe you could accompany me. So, shall we eat now that's all sorted?" he said finally ending his speech.

Later, Lucy lay in bed thinking: Here it was again another one of those moments where I end up wondering, *Did that all really just happen? A date, but not really a date, with more really-not-really dates in the future. Go spend on my credit card, because this one's for you! And things in the future.*

What things.

What's happening here?

You need to put more effort into looking for a proper job, she thought, *teaching music or art.* All this playing house and happy families isn't a wise idea. It was starting to get complicated – now she was a nanny and a dinner escort. And she wasn't prepared to be either long-term. This could all lead very much to heartbreak. Even if she was finding it a little exciting at the same time.

Somewhere in her subconscious whilst still lying in her bed, she heard Marcos' car pulling away down the gravel drive and couldn't help feeling a little disappointed that he hadn't offered to go shopping with her, as she really didn't know what was expected. *Might as well get up,* she thought, she was never going to sleep now. That moment had long passed with her restless mind everywhere. So she showered, got dressed and made herself a coffee before Dante stirred. Then after giving him his breakfast and getting him ready to go, they headed off in her little old car to take him to the nursery. After kissing and hugging him goodbye until later, she next headed into town with a view to shopping until she dropped, or at least until she found something she felt was suitable.

But three hours and half a dozen boutiques later, Lucy just wasn't getting the vibe. There were lots of beautiful dresses but nothing shouting out at her and it wasn't helping that she wasn't sure what she was even dressing for. She decided she definitely needed some help.

Marcos could hear his phone ringing and seeing her name on the screen, answered it quickly, asking, "Lucy, is everything all right?"

"Yes, Marcos. Dante is fine, if that's what you mean but I need you to help me with this shopping trip a bit. I can't shop when I don't know what I'm shopping for – I could end up showing us both up. I'm sure I've never been to anything like what you tell me we're going to."

Hearing the desperation in her voice, Marcos realised he really had been a little unfair expecting her know what was, and what he, expected of her. She had said clearly to him when he had asked her she had never been to such an occasion before.

"OK, where are you Lucy?" he asked.

"I'm in the main street in the town. There's a lot of gorgeous stuff here, Marcos, but there are so many different styles. I don't know what you are expecting of me," she said.

"OK – you go and get a coffee and I'll ring you when I get there. I just need to finish what I'm doing here. Give me, say, an hour."

"Thank you," she said. "I'm sorry but I just don't want to get this wrong."

"It's fine, Lucy. Though I'm sure you wouldn't have got it wrong anyway. But wait for me there and I'll see you shortly," he said before hanging up.

Three boutiques later, they were chatting away. They were, but weren't, employee and employer. She thought, no…they were so much more than that. She still couldn't deny how madly she was attracted to him, but if this was all she could have until it was time for her to leave, then this at least was better than nothing.

Two hours later, the shopping was done. And she had the most beautiful red, halter-neck evening gown with a long, flowing skirt which shimmered when it caught the light. To wear with it, she had a sheer cashmere wrap in matching red and extremely high-heeled silver diamanté sandals with one strap across the front of her toes that sparkled as she walked, and an ankle strap to keep them feeling secure, in case she thought and hoped they danced.

Marcos had insisted on booking appointments for her hair and nails, but she wanted to do her own makeup. He told her not to worry about jewellery. He would deal with that. And she couldn't help but smile at him, sheer happiness and excitement written all over her face, the daunting feelings of only hours earlier now completely faded away.

"OK, Lucy, I need to go back to the office for a few hours and I could be late so don't wait for me for supper tonight. But this afternoon has been worth it, so I'll maybe see you later and if not, then tomorrow night."

"OK, and thank you again, Marcos," she replied.

"No need to thank me. You're the one doing me the favour." And with that, he kissed her on the cheek and left.

Lucy decided to head off for Dante. It was nearly time. And although the traffic was heavy, she still arrived in plenty of time to spare.

He was such a happy little soul, throwing his little chubby arms around her neck and hugging her tight.

Once in the car and belted in, they set off back to the house, Lucy singing nursery rhymes and getting Dante to join in. Every day, morning and night, they did this – singing along together and his speech and learning were coming along tremendously for his age and all whilst they were having fun.

Back at the house, Lucy fed, bathed and played with the little man until it was his bedtime, then warmed up his milk and took him up for his bottle and story. It was the same routine every night and it worked well: a short story, then she would sing him a lullaby, whilst stroking his fringe away from his forehead. His dark, wavy hair framing his face, and large, dark eyes like molten saucers becoming glazed and slowly shutting, as he drifted away into a beautiful, peaceful sleep.

Making sure the monitor was switched on and then turning off the light, she went back downstairs. But it didn't feel right tonight – there was no smell of cooking, nobody to chat to, share dinner with or talk about the day over a glass of wine. It actually made her feel quite empty and lonely, and she realised she was missing Marcos and their shared evenings together. Yet only a few weeks before, she hadn't even known him. Going into the kitchen, Lucy switched on the kettle and put two slices of bread into the toaster. Tonight, she would simply have cheese on toast and a cup of tea, then maybe an early night. Sleep would be the best way to pass the evening.

"Hello," came the sound of a voice – his voice. "You look miles away," he was saying, standing in the doorway and observing her from a distance. For a moment Lucy was a little startled, then there seemed just no point in denying it. So, she simply came out with it. "I was just thinking about you and our evenings together," she said.

"My thoughts exactly," came his reply, "that's why I'm here."

She was holding her breath, yet even as she did so she could feel it being sucked out of her. Her heart wanted to let her scream out, *So you were missing me too*, but her words were lost as her breath was still caught in her throat as he crossed the room and took her in his arms, kissing her like his life depended on it. Their lips were locked, their tongues entwined and her heart pounding. She could feel her hands shaking as she lifted up her arms and wrapped them tightly around his neck, pulling him closer to her, at the same time as he was pulling her closer still to him. Their bodies pressed against each other, she could feel his erection long and hard pushing against the fabric of her clothes. Whilst her own body yearned for his touch, an ache so deep and needy, she thought she might cry out in despair. Their kissing felt endless, intoxicating like a drug, only stopping occasionally to draw breath. She felt his hands slip under her blouse whilst at the same time hers were pulling at his shirt. She wanted – she needed – to feel his body, feel his skin against her hands. She wanted him so much, but she needed him even more.

"Spend the night with me, Lucy," he said softly in her ear, his warm breath sending shudders down her spine. "I want you so much."

"Yes," was all she could manage, still clinging to him; her body trembling and weak from the kiss and the feel of his touch, leaving her wondering if she might fall to the ground if she dare to let go.

Voice hoarse, lips tracing their way down her neck, Marcos stopped and for a moment whilst gently holding her still and looking straight into her eyes he asked her again.

"Will you spend the night with me, Lucy?"

She knew he was giving her the chance to change her mind, to stop now before there was no going back, to be sure.

But she was sure, more than sure, of her answer. No regrets. Two adults wanting each other, longing to spend one less lonely night and enjoy the pleasures of each other and what the night would bring.

"I want to spend the night with you, Marcos. You. This is what I want," she replied.

Not another word was spoken. The air was thick with anticipation and their need was almost at boiling point. Hand-in-hand, they left the kitchen and headed towards the stairs. But once at the top, hesitation filled Lucy's head. Whose room where they going to? Her mind already telling her she didn't want it to be hers, if this night was to be special and this man wanted to take her to bed, then it must be his bed.

She was sure he must have been reading her thoughts or at least felt her hesitation and sudden insecurity as his hand tightened its grip and he pulled her closer to him. "My bed, Lucy, all night, and we'll be making love, not having sex."

She hadn't realised how tense she'd become until she felt her whole body relax and the uncertainty leave her as quickly as she'd felt it arrive. Lucy hadn't been inside his room before, she'd never even dared to peep inside. The door was always closed, and there had been no need for her to ever try to go beyond it.

Marcos had made her feel very welcome in his home he'd made her feel it was her home too, regardless of the fact it wasn't supposed to be a long-term plan. From the moment they had met, it had all been so easy. They had just fallen into a routine both day and night, him never treating her like the hired hand, so she'd had no reason or need to poke about to try and understand her employer better.

Marcos pushed open the door, never letting go of Lucy's hand. The room looked enormous. A king-size bed stood opposite the door and there must have been at least 10ft of floor space lying before it. Beautiful, tall, elegant lamps sat on mirrored bedside tables, with slim French doors on either side, dressed with exquisitely rich curtains hanging from the outer edge to allow extra light to filter into the room. The excess fabric lay lavishly on the floor, adding to the already stunning ambience of the room. Fitted wardrobes in dark oak, lined one wall. A dressing table and a large chest of drawers against another, whilst a snuggle chair and a small mirrored table sat near one of the French doors, looking out over the garden, making the view even more beautiful from up here. The walls were neither white nor cream, with a feature wall behind the bed in a charcoal grey, textured fabric wallpaper, the bedding was soft grey with throws and cushions on the bed and snuggle chair, in a combination of charcoal and silver. The room was undoubtably stunning and whoever had chosen it had extremely good taste.

"You like?" Lucy heard his words spoken softly in her ear and realised her mind had yet again been miles away.

"I like," was all she could manage in return. And suddenly, once again, there was no time for talking, only kissing. Standing behind her with his arms tightly wrapped around her waist, his lips gently kissed her neck as she felt her body pushing against him, her head straining upwards, so his lips could reach all and any part of her neck. She could feel the ache deep down inside her, the heat in her nipples as they screamed out for his touch, her breathing so erratic she felt she was gasping for air.

She didn't know how much longer she could stand it, feeling his erection pushing against his trousers, pushing against the barriers of their clothing and against her lower back. She wanted him, needed him, needed to touch and feel him, taste him. She didn't feel she could wait another moment. Turning into his arms, she wrapped her arms around his neck. One hand finding its way under his polo shirt where she could feel his skin whilst the other hand tangled its fingers in his hair. She heard him gasp and felt herself melt in his arms. Again, their lips found each other, deep and searching. Locked together in such a way Lucy felt for sure that there was no going back from this moment, and not a single breath in her body wanted to.

Pulling gently away from her yet never yet never letting go still holding her hand, Marcos slowly led her to the bed, gently pushing her down so she was sat on the very edge, before lowering himself and kneeling in front of her. And all Lucy could think was whatever he wanted to do to her, she was about to let him.

Slowly, he unbuttoned and removed her blouse, still kissing and caressing her whilst his hands continued to the zip on her trousers. Gently she felt them slip away from her body, the heat from his hands feeling like it was burning her bare skin as they stroked and caressed her. Finally, her delicate lace underwear followed. Suddenly naked, a moment's shyness passed over her. But at that very same moment, as if he too had felt it, Marcos held her in his arms and told her how beautiful she was, before laying her down on the bed and telling her that now he was going to show her how beautiful he thought her body was. He started by kissing her lips, but they soon moved on to trace their way to her neck sending shudders rippling through her body as they made their way slowly down to her breasts, his tongue playing with her nipples, sucking and nipping at them, making her back arch and the need inside her becoming more urgent with every second.

Still, he continued moving yet further down, kissing and stroking her stomach with his tongue until suddenly she gasped as his tongue reached and began gently stroking her most intimate and inner parts. A feeling of pure ecstasy sending her body climbing higher and higher up some imaginary mountain desperate to reach the top. She felt her hands were everywhere, grabbing at his shoulders then his hair, until at last he reached out, taking hold of her wrists whist her whole body pushed against him begging for more of this most beautiful, almost unbearable feeling that she'd never before experienced. Her breathing was fast and heavy and she knew she was spiralling out of control. She suddenly tried pushing him away, to pull him up against her; the feeling inside of her a mixture of pleasure and a fear of something new and unknown. Marcos stilled for a moment, allowing her mind to make its own decision. He released one hand and reassuringly touching her lips before he quietly whispered, "Relax and enjoy it, Lucy," before his tongue gently revisited her most intimate and feminine core. Then suddenly, it was upon her. She felt it rising like some beautiful out-of-body experience and couldn't help but cry out, now finally dragging him towards her, holding on to him with all her strength, not sure she'd ever be able to let him go ever again. He kissed her gently now and stroked her hair away from her forehead, quietly asking if she was OK.

"More than OK," was her simple reply. It was then that he slipped off his clothes revealing his erection, big and hard, his body beautifully bronzed, a mixture of natural Greek olive skin and gentle rays from the warmth of the sun. Her eyes were transfixed, and she found herself thinking that all she wanted was to make love with him, feel him deep inside of her.

Lowering himself on to the bed, he hovered above her before asking her one last time, "Are you sure, Lucy?"

And once again her reply to him was simply, "Yes Marcos, never have I been more sure about anything." And as if to reassure him this time, she gently pulled him down towards her where the need for words was no more, and the look they held between them was more than any words could say.

Their lips found lips so deep and sensual, whilst other parts of their bodies sought to find each other in the desperate need to become as one. Then suddenly, he was there again but this time it wasn't his lips nor his tongue, no, she could feel this time his errection so hard and needy, touching the outer edges of her softest most intimate place, nudging her, teasing her, making her want him more and more before thrusting himself deep inside her, her arms wrapping tightly around his neck, legs curling around his while her head and lips buried deep into his neck. They seemed to move together, joined only as one. It felt like this was always the way they were meant to be. Their bodies so perfectly in tune together. The passion between them way beyond anything she had ever experienced, wild and passionate, yet filled with emotion. He was so deep inside of her, yet still she wanted him deeper. Just as she felt he too wanted to be deeper inside of her, thrusting harder and harder, holding tight to each other. The passion was rising and the tension building; so perfectly made for each other. Then suddenly, finally, amid an explosion of pure ecstasy, Lucy could hear herself cry out as one final hard thrust sent them both over the edge, climaxing together and leaving them both breathless and exhausted. They lay quiet and still in each other's arms, Marcos drawing her closer still to him, tightening his arms around her. Both content in the aftermath of the most perfect lovemaking, yet in the quiet stillness of the moments that passed, Lucy could feel a mixture of tears as well as sleep about to wash over her. Never had she dreamt she could feel this way, so sexy and loved, so uncontrollably emotional that she wanted to crawl under his skin to get as close to him as possible. And yet she also felt if she wasn't careful she was going to cry all over him for the beautiful and happy way he'd made her feel. She thought it may be time she went back to her own room. After all, in a few hours she would be back in charge of a small child, but as she started to speak and move Marcos quickly placed a finger on her lips, followed by a gentle kiss saying, "No,

Lucy, I said all night and that's what I want. You here in my bed next to me. All night." And wrapping his arms tightly around her, she felt a single tear slowly escape down her cheek as she felt herself relax, snuggle into his body and quickly drifted off to sleep.

It felt like only minutes since they had closed their eyes when they were woken by the sound of a crying baby, before the alarm had even had a chance to do its job. Lucy jumped instantly out of bed and went to see to Dante. Marcos followed and after spending a few minutes with his son, he went off to shower, get ready and leave for work. There hadn't been time to talk about last night, though Lucy didn't think there was anything that needed to be said. She had no regrets. She only knew she longed for more, and emotionally she was now in serious trouble.

The morning routine had been easily achieved and Lucy and Dante were now in the car on their way to nursery, singing songs just like they did every morning. With her mind drifting to the fast approaching dinner party and she decided when she got back to the house, she would try the dress on again. It was a gorgeous dress and from the moment she had first tried it on, she had loved it. But trying it on again today with the glow in her cheeks from the memory off the night before, she knew this time she would feel far sexier and more feminine than ever before.

And now standing looking at herself in the mirror, she was right – that was just how she felt. Feminine, sexy and with a new confidence from somewhere deep within, which she couldn't help wonder had been created the night before. In fact, she was sure it had, and now regardless of what may or may not happen again, she wouldn't quite be the baby-minder borrowed for a dinner date anymore. She heard her phone ping and grabbed it, excited to see if it was a message from Marcos. It was, but just not one she wanted to see.

'Sorry Lucy. Got to work late tonight. Can't make it for supper so don't wait up. X'

Tears streamed down her face at such an overwhelming feeling of disappointment, her mind racing. Had he decided it was a mistake already? Did he regret what happened or was she just being over-sensitive? Maybe he was working late. *After all*, she thought, *he is the head of a multi-million-pound business*, but why not just phone her instead of sending a message. He could at least speak to her. The whole day turned into a drag but eventually it was time to pick up Dante. And by the time she had fed Dante, bathed him and put him to bed, she was emotionally drained, and as much as she wanted and needed to see him, she decided to just go up to bed. Her appetite had gone, and she couldn't face food so decided coffee and a bar of chocolate would do. She didn't hear him come home, the stress and the tears had finally sent her into a sound sleep and when she woke to the sound of the alarm, she discovered he'd been home but already gone again. The days that followed were all the same, and now the dinner party was almost upon them.

She decided today that enough was enough and she was going to message him to check that it was all still on. The answer was *yes,* they needed to leave at 6:30 pm and his mother would be arriving on Friday for the weekend. But somehow this still didn't help the way Lucy was feeling.

And so, on Friday, Katerina arrived mid-afternoon. Rose, Marcos' housekeeper, had taken care of everything, her just being no more than efficient as usual, but leaving Lucy feeling like she was a spare part at best. It wasn't that Rose set out to make her feel that way, it was just that Lucy didn't know where she fit in anymore after that night.

Katerina and Lucy spent an hour or so together with a coffee and got on really very well. She had told her Marcos nursed a broken heart but didn't go any further apart from one quick comment, when she'd said he was great in business but had been a fool in love. And now here they were. She'd been so excited about the dinner party but now it just felt like a sham. The hired hand being taken out to ward off any undesirable attention. Katerina, she soon discovered though, was very easy company, and said straight away she had no desire to interfere in their routine, so she must tell her what she wanted her to do, and when she wanted any free time.

But as the dinner party was on a Saturday and Lucy already had hair and nail appointments booked, then she really didn't need any free time, so she just invited her to join them in what they did and later when she went back out for Dante, Katerina went along with her.

Dante was delighted to see his grandma, running and throwing his arms around her, it was a real pleasure to see and made her realise what a big part of his life she was, and clearly had been, after the loss of his mother. After collecting him from nursery, they all went to the park, played on the swings and had ice cream. Katerina asked how she was finding living in and taking care of a small child, but it was easy chat, not a questionnaire and she felt sure there was no hidden agenda. And so, as the evening passed by, Katerina and Lucy ate supper together in the kitchen after Dante had gone to bed, after once again there had been another message from Marcos, saying he would be late.

She heard him come in after they'd retired to their rooms and vaguely heard voices, so assumed he and his mother were having a chat. But once again, she didn't get to see him, instead she just lay there wondering what tomorrow night would hold, leaving her stomach churning and a feeling of uncertainty. She almost wished she could come down with an illness and he could take someone else, even his mother, and she would babysit.

Suddenly, her phone bleeped and lit up. Marcos: a message.

Sorry, not going to be about all day tomorrow. Serious business issues. Hope you're OK? Everything is still good for tomorrow tonight. See you later. XX

And so, the next day passed – a long soak in the bath, followed by a visit to the nail bar, where Lucy decided on simple, short red nails with matching toes, to match the dress. Her next visit was to the hair salon, where she decided to have it curled, giving it a soft, sexy look, which could be clipped up at one side, revealing her earlobe and emphasising her neck. All in all, by 6:00 pm, she was actually feeling very glamorous and sexy in the beautiful red dress and high heels.

The heels were a little higher than she would definitely normally wear but she loved them. She was glad she'd decided to do her own makeup and was completely satisfied with the look of her smoky soft eyes and red lips. It felt good, even fabulous, to be dressed like this but it was just a little daunting at the same time. And she still hadn't seen Marcos. She knew he was now home and getting ready for the evening ahead, and she couldn't help wondering what the night may or may not bring. Glancing one last time in the large full-length mirror before deciding she must go downstairs, Lucy smiled as she was reminded herself of Cinderella, dressed in finery and excited to go, yet unsure if she was the one the prince would truly desire!

It was now 6.30 pm and time to leave the bedroom. She couldn't hide in there any longer; whatever would be, would be and she had to face it. Slowly, she started down the stairs taking extra care as such high heels weren't by any means her everyday thing. She held her wrap and clutch bag in one hand and slightly lifted the skirt of her dress with the other, so as not to catch it in her heels. She could see Marcos in his tuxedo, waiting for her in the hallway. The very sight of him took her breath away, and she couldn't help but wish she knew how he felt about her. As she approached the last few stairs, Marcos put out his hand and offered it to her. Lucy reached out and took it and although it should have been there to steady her, instead the connection between them was like electricity running through her veins, and she knew this feeling was never going to go away.

"You look beautiful, Lucy. You are absolutely stunning, though I think you need a little something around your neck," he said, "and I have just the thing." With that, he reached into the inner pocket of his jacket and took out a long-slim box, out of which he took a delicate gold necklace with a single solitaire diamond and carefully fastened it around her neck. The slight touch of his fingers on the bare skin of her neck sent a shudder of desire straight down to her core, but he wasn't finished. Next came a bracelet, a simple circle of diamonds encased in the same colour gold, the light from the

51

chandelier above catching the stones and making them gleam and sparkle. Her breath caught in her throat, and for all she tried, Lucy just didn't seem able to speak a single word.

"The bracelet is from Dante," he was saying, "and the necklace is from me, in appreciation of how much better you've made our lives since the very first day we met you." Still unable to utter a single word, Lucy could feel the tears welling up in her eyes as his gaze held her still. And any minute now, her makeup was about to be ruined.

"No tears, Lucy," he was saying, one hand gently touching the side of her cheek while he still stood so close she could feel his warm breath on her skin, "They were supposed to make you happy. They are gifts. And I'm sorry I've not been here all week. There was a crisis at work but I'm here now, and for tonight at least, I am all yours."

"I thought you'd changed your mind," she could hear herself saying, "and that you didn't want me," she whispered.

"That couldn't be further from the truth, Lucy," was his reply, drawing her close into his arms. As the tension left her body, replaced with the overwhelming urge to sob all over him with relief. She could still feel his breath warm against her ear as he held her close and whispered softly, how truly sorry he was that he just hadn't realised.

Marcos had decided they would be chauffeur driven for this evening, allowing them both to relax and enjoy the wine. Although it was an important business evening for him, it was also a dinner date for them too and for that reason he wanted them both to enjoy it. And so, the evening had begun, they were on their way for what Marcos said would only be a very short journey. And it had definitely felt like it because they had chatted and laughed during the whole time, as Marcos took hold of her hand gently in his, slowly tracing its palm with his thumb and sending unimaginable thoughts through her mind that she dare not dwell upon. The car slowed and pulled up outside the venue, a very large, well-lit, extremely impressive mansion. Suddenly Lucy felt the butterflies in her stomach as the immense realisation that she was actually Marcos' date for the evening, sank in.

He must have sensed it, felt her apprehension as her mind said is it too late to run, because he gently squeezed her hand and said, "You look beautiful, Lucy, and you're here because I asked you, and there is nobody I'd rather have here with me tonight."

But once inside the doorway, the whole impact of the evening once again hit her. She could feel the eyes of various guests taking a good look at her and couldn't help but wonder what he had told them. Now she felt a little ridiculous that she hadn't given it a thought to ask him. She felt the heat of his hand searing through the delicate fabric of her dress, making the hairs on the back of her neck tingle and the sensation ripple down her spine as it rested on the lower part of her back. He slowly guided her forwards, suggesting they went and got themselves a drink then mingle with the other guests. She felt aghast. The mansion was enormous, not the kind of place she was at all used to with its huge, shimmering chandeliers, magnificent spiral staircase, waiters with trays of champagne and so many guests; the men all in tuxedos, while the women dressed in all their elegance, beautiful gowns, jewellery and all that went with them. And who was she, thought Lucy, Cinderella, longing for the clock to strike midnight, then she could take flight and run, because right at this moment that was all she desired to do. She could feel the eyes of so many other beautiful women wondering who she was and how did she get to be Marcos' date. At that very thought she felt she could actually laugh out loud at what their faces would look like if they only knew she was really no more than the baby-minder, albeit the baby-minder who had shared the most amazing night of passion with him.

By the time midnight came, Lucy was no longer worried about fleeing from the party. The evening had been wonderful, with great, easy company in the dining room, and delicious food and wine. But the ultimate part of the evening was definitely when Marcos had held her in his arms and they had waltzed around the dance floor. That feeling of being held in his arms whilst he held her close and the music played was as romantic as she could ever have imagined it could be, and once again she could have cried all over him. But that was maybe for what she wanted it to be and not for what it was. She so wished this was a real date, to be the woman and only woman in his life, holding each other close while the music made them gently sway in each other's arms.

The journey towards home was quiet. The wine and the ambiance of the evening leaving them both relaxed and a little tired. Sat together once again in the back of the limousine, her head resting on his shoulder, Marcos again held her hand, as her thoughts silently spiralled a round in her head, *What now?* and, *Then what?* But she was too scared of the answer to ask the questions, and it wasn't long before the car slowed and turned towards the big wrought iron gates.

Suddenly, the chauffeur raised his voice and spoke quickly to Marcos, "Sir, the gates are already open. And look! A police car is at the house." Marcos quickly jumped out of the limousine not waiting for the driver to finish the journey to the house and dashed across the driveway towards the front door. "Don't panic, Marcos," Katerina already there was calling out to him. "I called the police as a precautionary measure."

"Why? What has happened?" Marcos asked in an anxious and slightly raised voice.

"Sir," the policeman said politely but firmly while interrupting. "Your mother thought she heard a voice outside, and thought she saw a shadow in the grounds, so she called us to be on the safe side. We've checked over the grounds and all around the house, but all seems to be in order. Would there be any reason maybe she would think this?"

Marcos thought for a minute, but then assured the police officer that he could think of no reason. But when morning came, he said he would add to the security of the house and grounds as a precautionary measure anyway. And not long after this and after a final walk around the grounds, the officers finally left, leaving the three of them in the kitchen, Katerina and Lucy both sat at the breakfast bar while Marcos too agitated to sit, stood, having now acquired the brandy pouring each off them a large amount, saying it would help them to relax and sleep. Katerina explained how she'd thought she'd heard a noise, a plant pot knocked over maybe and possibly the lightest crunch of a footstep on the gravel driveway. It had been enough to make her get out of bed and peep out of the window, staying hidden behind the curtains and that's when she thought she'd seen a shadow. "But maybe," she said, "I had just been tired."

"Maybe," said Marcos. "But let's keep our eyes and ears open, just in case. This is a little more real than any of us would care to think." They all drank the rest of their brandy in silence. Each, Lucy was sure, was lost in his or her own thoughts.

"Was there someone in the garden? How, if there was, had they got in? And why?"

All the romance of the evening had been spoilt, and with good reason. The emotion and the anticipation had all been lost in a much more serious and worrying moment. And it had suddenly become just time for bed.

When the dawn finally came, Lucy wondered if anybody had actually managed to get any sleep, or if, like her, they had tossed and turned for what seemed like all night long asking themselves if there really had been an intruder and what might have happened had Katerina not heard a noise, leaving their minds full of questions but empty of answers. Maybe the new day would shed some light on to it all, she thought, and though it was still very early she decided she might as well just get up, shower and dress. She climbed out of bed and headed to the bathroom, peeping out of the window into the garden as she did so. It was still dark the sun had not yet started to rise and with the thought of the night before an early feeling shuddered over her, *Had there been somebody out there last night?* She showered pulled on some leggings, a vest top and a loose blouse, doubting that after last night's scare anybody would be going far today. Then she headed off to the kitchen where she found Marcos on his phone already and it was very clear to see he had been there for some time. Empty coffee cups and pieces of paper with writing on lay on the breakfast bar; he looked tired with dark circles of worry having appeared around his eyes while his hair looked like his hands had been through it countless times. She wondered if he had actually been to bed and seriously doubted it as she heard him talking on his mobile again to the police, telling them he was arranging extra security cameras, checking locks and various other things. Seeing her enter the kitchen, he walked over from the other side, gently squeezed her hand and planted a soft, gentle kiss on her lips before returning his attention back to the person on the other end of the telephone. Speaking both in Greek and English the conversation was fast, with a tone of real authority in Marcos's voice. She could tell he was giving someone extremely strict orders regarding more outside security lighting, cameras and changing the locks; this really had shaken him up.

Once off the telephone, Marcos told Lucy that his mother would now be staying on for a few days. He thought it best she had a little extra support to be on the safe side. He'd also ordered Lucy a new car, feeling it would be safer and more reliable right now. And for the time being he didn't want her going to the parks, shops or anywhere else on the way to or from the nursery and she must speak to him regularly throughout the day. He was clearly distressed about the whole situation and she couldn't help but wonder whether he now wished he'd had that DNA test done just in case there became more questions to answer.

The days slipped by and all seemed normal, although Marcos still didn't want them going back to their old routine yet and Katerina seemed unable to go home. As for Lucy, she had now received a beautiful, but not needed in her opinion, Mercedes, and she now spoke to Marcos endless times in the day. That was, in her opinion, at least one positive amongst so many negativities but the sad side was they hadn't progressed either, or talked or anything, and she was left wondering if she was now just the baby-minder again and maybe she should be realistic and just move on.

Two weeks after that eventful night, Katerina decided she would go home but would return immediately if she was needed at any time. Rose, who had been staying late and cooking the evening meal, had been told by Marcos that she may return to her usual duties. And though she would still often prepare a meal, she was usually now be long gone before it was cooked and so it was back to just them, but just who were *they*?

Employer and employee?

Master and baby-sitter?

Two people playing happy families, not yet sure what the next move would be?

Lucy didn't really know what she should do. Cook dinner? Go to bed? Ring and ask – or wait to be told? It was 7:30 pm and Dante was fast asleep, already fed and bathed and they'd had a little story and sing-along, during which he had fallen asleep. He looked so peaceful lay there stretched out in the warm night air, thumb in his mouth, his dark wispy hair starting to wave at the ends and his little chubby hands and feet looking even cuter now they were slightly tanned from their earlier trips to the park. Lucy couldn't help but just sit there in the chair by the side of his cot and look at the pure innocence and perfection of such a beautiful happy toddler. Thank God life events didn't seem to have left any permanent scars.

"Lucy, Lucy."

She could hear a quiet voice saying her name but couldn't quite find the person in her dream. "Lucy." There it was again. Suddenly, she opened her eyes, and realised Marcos was standing over her.

"What?" she asked. "What is it?"

"You're asleep in the chair in Dante's room. Come on, you need to go to bed and get some sleep."

Taking her hand to make sure she got out of the chair Marcos gently led her out of Dante's room, where he stopped and asked, "Your room or mine, Lucy?"

For a moment, she was too dazed and half-asleep to even think but then she thought she felt too tired and emotional to dare spend what could be another amazing night of passion with him when she still had no idea if he had any real feelings for her at all. So she simply answered, "Mine, Marcos.

Because I'm starting to feel like a dirty secret. Good night." She left him standing there as she went into her room and closed the door. But lying in her bed now, unable to catch her sleep, all she could ask herself was why she hadn't just gone to his bed? She knew how she felt about him and alone here isn't where she wanted to be, but again she reminded herself of the reason. The more time she spent with him the deeper she could feel herself falling in love with him. But for him, she may be no more than a few convenient nights of passion until he found himself a permanent nanny and then Lucy would be gone. Finally, she gave up tossing and turning, it was just no use, she'd barely eaten for the last twenty-four hours so now she was hungry and sleepless. Hot milk and chocolate it would have to be, so she quietly went downstairs and once in the kitchen, put a mug of milk into the microwave and found a large bar of milk chocolate in the fridge. She'd forgotten how much she actually loved hot milk and cold chocolate. It had always been a real comfort to her in her teenage years and was definitely worth getting out of bed for. She was feeling much better already, sitting quietly and enjoying them both until the main light flashed on and a voice that could only be Marcos shouted: "Who the hell is there? Show yourself."

"For Christ's sake, Marcos, it's me," she yelled and burst into tears at the same time as she finally reached the 'can't take anymore' stage. Realising instantly it was Lucy and cursing under his breath, Marcos rushed over, pulling her into his arms and holding her close, whispering in her ear how truly sorry he was and explaining that he'd thought it was an intruder. Now slowly they both started to relax again, but he could have been talking about anything, as right at that moment Lucy couldn't stop crying. And now it was turning into sobs that she just couldn't stop. She could hear his voice in her ear against the dampness of her tear-soaked hair, "Tell me, Lucy. What is making you cry like this?" he asked as he wiped away her tears and gently kissed her forehead.

"I'm OK," she said, wiping her face with her hands and trying to smile. "It's just all got a bit too much, and I was tired and hungry but I'm fine now," she answered. "Time I went back to bed, it will soon be time get up."

"Sleep with me tonight, Lucy, and yes, I mean sleep. I don't want you to be alone tonight, and neither do I think you do. I want you in my bed, so I can hold you close to me all night and then tomorrow night when I get home, we will talk."

Still holding her firmly in his arms waiting for her answer, Lucy was lost. It was all she wanted and needed to hear him say, all she thought she would ever want. Just him. So this time she said yes and taking his hand in hers she led him from the kitchen to his bedroom. She could feel herself drifting away, a wave of exhaustion washing over her. She lay semi-naked wearing only his t-shirt. She had been shivering so much by the time they'd undressed, from a mixture of tiredness and emotion, that he'd taken his t-shirt off and slipped it straight over her head. She could smell his aftershave, the woody, spicy and intoxicating aroma filling her senses and playing tricks with her mind and body. The t-shirt was still warm from his body, making it comforting and sexy both at the same time. Marcos drew her down under the bedcovers and they were cocooned together, his bare chest pressed against her back, his arms tightly wrapped around her, their legs curled around each other, joining them together perfectly as if they were one. It felt so natural, so complete like this was the way they should fall asleep every night, always to be together.

Lucy opened her eyes and realised she hadn't been dreaming and that yes, she was in Marcos' bed. A thought flashed through her mind of how good it had felt as she'd drifted off to sleep wrapped in his arms. But now she was awake and wondering why she was alone. A wave of sadness came over her and her heart sank, before deciding rather than risk facing him she would get out of his bed now and quickly go back to her own room. But before she'd even got her two feet on the ground, Marcos appeared in the doorway carrying a very tearful Dante and saying, "Here we are. Here's Lucy."

"I'm so sorry, Marcos," Lucy heard herself saying. "You must need to get ready for work. Pass Dante to me, and we'll go to one of our own rooms."

"Stay there, Lucy. The time is fine. Let's have five minutes of family time before the day gets started." Hope filled her heart and with that, suddenly all three of them were back in bed, with Dante cuddling up to her, wrapping his chubby little arms around her neck. As Marcos reached out and took hold of her hand, she could feel a tear rolling down her cheek as she thought of the love she felt for them and the family they almost were.

After what could only be described as a perfect start to any day, Marcos had showered and left for work and she and Dante were almost ready to leave for Nursery. She was just about to grab her purse and keys on the way out, when the house phone rang. Lucy stopped and grabbed it quickly, answering, "Hello," but was left with a strange and uneasy feeling when nobody spoke. A feeling of worry came over her as she couldn't help but wonder if again maybe they we're being watched, or was the idea just now in her imagination after that night? Who would want to do that – and for what reason? She thought maybe she should phone or text Marcos, or could it wait as they were now almost running late? No, she decided she would ring him, but when she tried his phone it was engaged, and she didn't want to leave a message. So she decided she would try again after dropping Dante off. No need to panic him by leaving a message that may sound complicated and get misunderstood.

The easy perfect morning was now turning into a mad rush. Rose was having the day off for her daughter's graduation, and now Lucy was feeling a bit on edge being at the house alone after the phone call. Marcos still hadn't called her back and it had now been at least ten minutes, Rose was normally there to see them off so Lucy wasn't used to locking up and that, she realised, now had made her life so much easier.

Now in the car and ready for off, they were fine. They were running a little late, but it would all be fine. Dante was strapped in his seat and Lucy was all set to drive off when she glanced back at the house and saw the front door wasn't shut. How could that be? She knew she had definitely shut the door yet she could see it was now half-open. "No way," she said out loud, while sighing to herself and thinking, *For goodness' sake,* as she unfastened her seatbelt and jumped out of the car to go and slam the door shut. She was still sure she had pulled it tight shut; *That's the problem with old wooden doors,* she thought.

"OMG! No, no, no!" she could hear herself screaming; her hand still on the door knob as she watched her car speed away with Dante strapped in his baby seat. She couldn't stop screaming, but somewhere she could also hear a ringing sound. Realising it was her phone in her pocket and it must be Marcos finally calling her back, Lucy grabbed it, answering it at the same time. She was crying and yelling and making she knew, very little sense, but she just couldn't get control.

"Lucy! Lucy! What's happened? Tell me now," Marcos was saying. But Lucy was just hysterical at the other end of the phone. Suddenly, Marcos yelled back at her, "Lucy stop now. Stop now, and explain calmly to me what has happened?"

Sobbing down the phone, she tried to relay what had just happened, she could hear his silence and feel him go stony cold, whilst simply saying, "I'm hanging up now Lucy, and calling the police. I'm on my way. Just stay where you are."

It felt like forever while Lucy waited for Marcos and the police to arrive. Marcos had arrived first, his car speeding up the drive, his face so ashen it was the colour of death. The police were only moments behind. But what could she tell any of them? It had all happened so fast. It was so unreal, and she just simply couldn't stop crying, Marcos sat quietly, holding her hand as the policewoman asked questions.

What happened?

What did she see?

Tell us about the phone call?

Lucy told her everything she could. But it just seemed to be so little. She hadn't heard a voice or seen a person, and it had all happened so fast. And Dante, poor baby Dante must be so afraid. Who had taken him, and why? She felt it was just all her fault."

Thank God Dante hadn't been kidnapped in her old car. Only days ago, Marcos had the beautiful four-door white Mercedes delivered, telling her that although he knew she loved her old car, this would be safer, far more reliable and one less worry for him. It was undoubtedly a beautiful car and although she'd protested, he had insisted and she had to agree that hers was old and a little temperamental at times, and this one was beautiful and a pleasure to drive. Though it had more gadgets than she thought she would ever know what to do with, she now couldn't help wondering if the car itself had maybe attracted attention. Nobody seemed to look twice at them before. But who could say at this moment in time and at least the Mercedes had a tracking device fitted to it which the police could trace. But what was making her feel worse was how easy she'd made it for the kidnapper to get away. She had just pressed the in-car control for the electric gates to open when she had noticed the front door. The policewoman was very calm and understanding in asking her questions and appeared no way judgemental in what had happened, yet Lucy still couldn't help but keep thinking: *Does she think I might have some part in all this?* It felt like it was all getting worse by the minute.

Marcos was now telling the police that the car had a tracking device, and that he had already phoned the company who had fitted it, and they were on the phone ready to speak to the police. And so it went on, Marcos asked the same questions as the police, and the police asked the same questions again, but Lucy just didn't have any answers. It had all happened so fast. She kept replaying it back again and again but it just wasn't getting any clearer. She'd fastened Dante in the car. The front door was shut, or so she thought. She was in the car and pressed the remote for the gates to open and as she glanced behind, that's when she saw the front door was open. So, she reversed, jumped out of the car, ran to the door and that's when and how it had happened. He, or whoever it was, had just jumped into the car and driven off.

Some hours later, sat silently in the kitchen, Katerina and Pablo arrived, both grief-stricken, both too with ashen faces, both hugging Marcos and then Lucy, whilst asking if they were alright and if there was any more news. A police officer remained at the house. After all, Marcos was an important businessman, and it was expected a ransom would be demanded sometime soon. Marcos was clearly out of his mind with worry. He looked terrible and had hardly spoken a word to Lucy since it had all happened, although he had been supportive when the police had needed to speak to her and comforted her when he'd arrived. But now she had a feeling deep inside of her that he blamed her, maybe not that he wanted to, more that he just needed to blame someone and she had been the only person there so it had to be her. It was the worst feeling she could ever have imagined feeling, the thought that this man who she was in love with would think she could possibly do something to endanger a child, his child. A child she loved as much as if he were her own. Silent tears trickled down her cheeks, despair filling her heart along with utter sadness and misery.

Suddenly, the silence and tension in the room was shattered as the phone belonging to the senior officer still at the house and assigned to the case, began ringing. Not another sound could be heard in the room other than him replying to what was being said at the other end of the telephone. Everyone else in the room held their breath, watching, waiting and wanting to scream out, "Tell me. Tell me. What's happening?"

The officer hung up and calmly lifting his hands announced, "Dante is safe and well. The car has been found and the person believed to be responsible has been arrested. I advise you to go to the hospital, they are taking Dante there now as we speak, but it's just a precautionary measure for a check-up. The relief flowed through them almost drowning them with joy and happiness at the news, with hugs and tears being all that anyone could manage at that moment. They were all too emotional and relieved to speak.

Then Marcos spoke first, suggesting he set off straight away to the hospital. Lucy, suddenly finding her voice asked if she could go with him and with the gentlest of smiles, he replied, "Of course." His reply made her wonder if she had perhaps just imagined the way she thought he'd felt about her, brought on by the stress of the whole situation. He was busy now, assuring his mother and Pablo that once they were there and had a better picture of what was going on, he would phone straight away, but maybe just for now it would be best if only two of them went and they stayed at the house, in case the police wanted to speak again to anyone.

The journey seemed endless, yet it was only a couple of miles away. After today's scare, Lucy was busy thinking she couldn't do this anymore, but after today she was also thinking Marcos maybe wouldn't want her to anyway. Although his response to her coming along had been warm and he'd agreed with the idea immediately, the air now seemed to have changed and the distance between them felt so great; it felt unreachable. She had no idea what he was thinking as he was silent with only his own thoughts, yet twenty-four hours earlier she would have said they were very much in tune with each other.

There was definitely something going on in his mind, something he was not yet willing to share. The hospital car park was full, and the minutes felt like hours in the desperate, frustrating search for a space. Eventually Marco's spied a space and quickly parked the car, and they were off running towards the hospital's main entrance. The police officer had told them that they had taken Dante straight to the baby ward and that another officer had been assigned to wait there until Marcos had at least arrived and Dante had been given the all-clear.

Once in the lift and heading up to the main ward, Marcos suddenly looked at her as if just remembering she was there and asked, "Are you OK?"

"I will be, once I see Dante and know he's OK," Lucy replied. Marcos just nodded at that and she knew he was thinking the same.

Arriving at the baby unit the door was locked. It was a secure unit and they had to buzz and wait to be allowed inside. It was a good thing, security how it should be, but everything felt like it was taking forever because they were desperate to be inside. A nurse appeared and before Marcos could even open his mouth to speak, she released the door, obviously fully aware of who he was.

She introduced herself as the staff nurse in charge and led the way straight to a side room, where they found another nurse holding a sad and tearful Dante and a police officer hovering around the doorway.

On sight of each other, one sad and frightened little boy was desperately reaching out to get to his daddy, whilst one frightened and very choked father was equally desperate to hold his son in his arms. *A terrible reason for such a reaction, yet a beautiful sight to see*, thought Lucy. So much unconditional love between this man and his son and yet, not too long ago, he was fighting these emotions for fear of this bond, too scared of the consequences he might have to face. But love has the power to fill your heart, and as for everything else, they just have to be dealt with a little at a time.

A gentle tap was heard on the door and as it started to slowly open, they saw the familiar face of the police officer who had been at the house earlier. He stepped inside the room, looking straight at Lucy whilst apologising to Marcos for the poor timing of the interruption. They heard him say there were unfortunately a few questions he needed to ask that couldn't wait, but hopefully wouldn't take too long to clear up.

"Is there a problem?" Marcos asked the officer, a look of worrying concern shadowing his face.

"It's fine," said Lucy, "although I did tell you and the female officer all I knew about what happened at the time."

"It's a little more complicated than that," replied the officer. "And maybe down at the station would be best."

"Pardon?" Lucy said, "What do you mean?"

"Do you know a Nikos Vasilis?" the officer asked.

"Yes, he's my ex-boyfriend. Why do you ask?"

"Well," replied the police officer, "It is he who has been arrested for car-jacking and kidnapping, so if you would please come along with me, I'm sure we will soon get this matter sorted out."

Lucy couldn't believe what she was hearing, but worse still was the look she was seeing on Marcos's face, one of complete disbelief and loathing.

She was about to say, "Please, Marcos, you surely can't believe I had anything to do with this." But her eyes were burning with tears and her throat closed, while her heart was pounding so hard she felt it was stopping her breathing. And there it was again, that feeling, that look on his face, that he doubted her.

Down at the station, the questions just seemed endless.

How long had she known Nikos?

When were they last in touch?

Did she know he was in town?

And on they went.

Four hours later, they said she was free to go, with no charges pressed, and they had been satisfied that she neither knew nor had anything to do with the incident.

It seemed Nikos had decided to come and find her, to give them, in his words, "another chance" but he had found her at the big house, assumed she'd fallen lucky and a rich man had fallen for her, whilst he was on his arse as usual, with no money and no real job, still avoiding living in the real world. He had become jealous and outraged at what he'd thought was her new-found life.

He'd thought she'd had it all: house, car, money and all for sleeping with a rich man and looking after his child, not even needing to look for a real job.

Tomorrow morning Nikos would appear in court, and while she was now free to go, Lucy didn't know where she *could* go. She wasn't really sure anymore after this, Marcos wouldn't want her back at the house or want her looking after Dante.

The look on his face had said it all. Although she knew none of this was her fault and she loved them both, the end had come, and she knew that too.

She could neither face going back to prove it nor wanted to. The rejection would just be too much. There was no real reason for him to make her feel judged or punished, yet after seeing that look in his eyes, she knew he already had done so by association. Lucy wandered outside into the still warm night air, a slight breeze blowing around her, as if trying to help blow away the day's events and suddenly, the whole last twenty-four hours of emotions caught up with her, and she found herself leaning against the surrounding wall of the police station, sobbing her heart out.

After what seemed like an eternity of uncontrollable, unstoppable crying, Lucy managed to call her mother, Eleanor, and she and Steffos came straight away to collect her. Her mum being mum, she didn't ask any questions but just held her daughter tight whilst she cried, shushing her and telling her not to worry; that it would all be all right and work itself out eventually. Steffos drove the car in silence, apart from the odd mutter under his breath. When the car slowed and stopped, Lucy realised they'd arrived at their house, their home. But the reality for Lucy was that it wasn't her home or her house, she didn't actually have a house or a home of her own and so nowhere felt like home to her now. Slowly, the tears began again to slip down her cheeks. How had life got so messy, she wondered. And yet she couldn't help but feel that it wasn't actually through any fault of her own either. Marcos, to her knowledge, hadn't been in touch, but at some point in the not too distant future, she knew she would have to go and collect her things, put a final end to it, there would be no reason to try and stay in touch. Dante would soon forget her, a new nanny would see to that, and the sooner she started to rebuild her own life the better, but at this moment she didn't feel ready to face that yet, she was too upset and angry and she didn't know which she felt more to care about any of it. She still couldn't shake the thought from her mind that Marcos could think she was capable of such a thing. It almost made her want to hate him now, and with that thought at least the tears were now stopping. But the real fact was – she still loved him.

Hours had slipped on by. Her eyes were sore with crying and her head ached from thinking of all that had happened. It was a mess. Where did she go from here? Where *could* she go from here? She didn't even have a job now!

Her mum suggested she go up to her old room, maybe take a shower and try and get some sleep as it was already now nearly 9:00 pm. The day had just slipped away and although it seemed like the best idea, Lucy wondered how she would ever be able to sleep after all that had happened.

Steffos had looked so concerned. He was a wonderful stepfather. Not a word or accusation had passed his lips, yet she felt many times he must have thought, *"How did you end up in this mess, Lucy? We tried to tell you years ago about that loser, Nikos. "* Instead, he merely smiled and said, "It will get better in time, and in the meantime just stay with your mum and me.

"We both love you very much, and you can take all the time you need to sort yourself out."

What a kind and considerate man he was! He had married a woman with grown up children and never once had he tried to push his opinion on them. He truly loved her mother, and they had a great mutual respect for each other, something Lucy hoped one day she might find for herself in a man.

Smiling at her not answering, Steffos simply added, "Sorted then, at least for the time being anyhow. Now what about you go and take a shower then have something to eat?"

So Lucy went off for a shower and then borrowed some PJs from her mum. Also borrowing her hairdryer, blasting the hot air over her clean hair. It didn't help how she felt on the inside but at least now showered and clean on the outside, she felt a little better and had washed away the stuffy smell of the police station together with a little of the dirt thrown at her in the awful day's events. Then, taking a deep breath, she decided to go back downstairs.

Back in the kitchen, Lucy found her mum and Steffos having a cup of coffee. On seeing her, her mum said how much better she looked while Steffos asked if she was ready to eat now.

"Coffee and an omelette, I think, for you, young lady, now you're back with us. She really didn't feel she could eat a thing, yet she knew she really needed to. So, reluctantly but gratefully, she agreed. And Steffos set about making a fresh pot of coffee and the omelette, while she and her mum both chose to sit there quietly, maybe not physically exhausted but mentally drained. It had turned out to be an awful day, with most definitely more awful days yet to come Lucy was sure. She needed time to heal, time to go and get her possessions back and then move on. Eleanor reached out and put her hand over Lucy's, before quietly suggesting that maybe tomorrow she should just get it over with, go to the house and get her stuff, not let it drag on. But Lucy wasn't ready to go there yet, and she certainly didn't feel ready to face Marcos. Not that it should have been an issue, everything had now been cleared up by the police, and there was no reason for her to feel guilty or for him to be difficult with her. He didn't even need to be there when she went, she would only need Rose to let her in whilst she collected her things and it would be the end, the final goodbye.

She just needed a little time to get her head around that part first. She hadn't done anything wrong, she told herself again, no matter what he thought.

Steffos made a beautiful omelette, light and fluffy and the smell of fresh coffee and hot, buttery toast should have been enough to tempt anyone, but Lucy's appetite had completely gone and all she could manage was to pick at it.

The calmness of the room, the support of her mum and Steffos, the loss she felt, the hurt and the feeling of being let down by the man she knew she loved, but who neither loved her in return or could even bear to be in the same room as her, was tearing Lucy apart. And suddenly, the tears were there again, and she found herself with her head in her hands, sobbing again. Steffos quietly left the room, leaving Eleanor to console her daughter, gently rubbing her back whilst she once again tried to pull herself together. Eleanor hushed her gently and told her to just let it out. It would all work itself out in the end and be OK. And although Lucy felt like it would never be OK again, the love and faith her mum had in her made her feel she would at least survive it. Sometime later, after the tears had subsided and a few smiles had appeared, Lucy went up to bed, back in her old room. Lying in the darkness between the cool cotton sheets, it felt strange. The different noises of the house to the one she'd become used to, and even more so, no baby to love or listen out for, or no feeling of waiting in anticipation of what may happen. She lay there and listened to the quietness, while the turmoil and mixed up emotions continued in her head.

Had Marcos not felt any of the things she'd felt – the chemistry, the anticipation? Had he ever really enjoyed her company? Had he enjoyed their times together? Or had she just been a way to pass some lonely hours, whilst she was looking after his child. Had he not have any real feelings for her or had she been merely a simple, easy opportunity?

Her mind was going over everything again and again, asking questions and finding no answers. Marcos had made no effort to find out how she was or to speak to her about what had happened, and the more she thought now that he could possibly think she would put his child in danger or be a part of what had just happened, the angrier she felt. And the angrier she felt, the faster more tears flowed down her cheeks as she drifted off to sleep.

Lucy couldn't say what she thought had started to wake her, the feeling that she wasn't sure she'd really been asleep at all, or maybe just the natural daylight forcing its way through the outer edges of the blinds. But either way, her eyes were determined they wanted to open, whether she was ready to face another day yet or not, and so she lay there wondering what it would bring. Or if it would bring anything at all.

She was there but felt not really of any value or importance to anyone. And after lying there for some minutes more, she decided feeling sorry for herself wasn't the answer and her mum was right, she would indeed be OK. She must stay positive as this wasn't her fault, and she needed to get sorted out and move on. But firstly, she needed to arrange to get her things back from Marcos's house. Secondly, she needed to seriously attempt to get a proper job, and thirdly, she needed a place of her own, so she could make a fresh start, wipe the slate clean and put this down to experience and then put it all behind her.

Stepping out of bed, she decided coffee would be the best thing to start the day and so she made her way to the kitchen. The house was so quiet, but of course, it would be. There was no baby in this house, and with that thought she could feel her stomach go into knots as she thought about them and how their morning would be without her there. She could smell fresh coffee while going towards the kitchen and there she found Steffos, who as always was pleasantly smiling. He greeted her by saying good morning and offering her a cup, which Lucy accepted gratefully whilst scanning the room. "Where's Mum?" she asked.

She could feel the look of horror written on her face as she absorbed the words coming out of Steffos' mouth.

"Erm… Your mother has gone to work."

"My mother has gone to work!" she repeated back to Steffos a little louder than was maybe necessary or she intented, whilst staring wide-eyed and trying to stay calm.

"Yes," he repeated. "Your mother has gone to work. She said she will say the same thing to Marcos that she said to me and that I am about to say to you, if you ask why she's gone to work"

"And that is?" she asked.

"You've been a fool. He is a fool and she doubts things are far from over between the two of you. So until then, everyone else should try not to act foolish and at least attempt to get on with being normal."

All Lucy could manage by way of a response as she picked up her coffee and headed back to her room was a rather subdued, "OK."

Arriving at the office much later than normal, Marcos was shocked to see Eleanor sat at her desk, busy working away. He felt more than a little apprehensive as he headed towards her saying, "I don't think I was expecting to see you here this morning Eleanor, but I'm glad you are."

"Why, Marcos? Have you judged us all on Niko's behaviour, or did you think we were all involved in some form of set up?"

"Eleanor, NO! I'm sorry – it was all just a massive shock and it got so muddled up and messy so fast."

Letting out a big sigh, and looking directly at Marcos Eleanor simply replied, "Lucy would never, ever have put Dante in danger, Marcos, and I think deep down you know that. But if you thought for one moment that such a thing would have been at all possible or in any scheme of things, then you need your head tested. Or taking to one side and shooting."

Marcos stood silent for a moment, a furrow appearing on his forehead as he seemed to digest what Eleanor had just said to him. Eventually he asked, "Is Lucy alright?"

Becoming very still and giving Marcos a defiant don't you dare as only a mother could look, Eleanor said in a stern, calm voice, "I'm here as your secretary, Marcos, and that is exactly what I'm doing now. I'm not here to fill in your questionnaire about my daughter who you've left in pieces and who, I might add, was actually doing you a favour when she agreed to be your temporary nanny. If you really want to know how she is, I suggest you ask her yourself – that's if you either care or can be bothered. Now, was there anything else?"

Sitting at his desk, head in his hands, Marcos felt like he'd been there before, filled with despair at the hands of a woman. But Lucy wasn't like any other woman he had known, and his behaviour, he supposed, had been selfish. No, on reflection he admitted there was no supposed about it. He *had* been totally selfish, and not once had Lucy complained. He'd asked her to look after his child in his hour of need, admittedly with good pay, but with no prospects. He'd asked her to put her life on hold, he had seen the bond his son and Lucy were forming and the relationship he was forming with her. They'd shared meals and shared leisure time. God! They'd even shared the most passionate night he'd ever had in his life, but not once had he told her how he felt about her or asked her about her feelings or what she wanted. No. He'd taken it all for granted, *her* for granted, let the days roll into weeks and so on, never thinking they would end, or they would run out of tomorrows. And now, here they were. Or rather, here *he* was in a mess again, but a different kind of mess, and he needed to stop and think about what he really wanted and how to achieve it. His mother had hardly spoken to him since the whole incident, angry that he hadn't gone to the police station, trusted in her and supported her. She'd told him to get a good lawyer ready, in case Lucy needed one. She'd had every faith in her and thought she was the best thing that had happened to her son and grandson. Katerina had tolerated Alyssa but in her own mind, she'd always thought she had seduced her son, married him for his money and the lifestyle he could offer rather than because she truly loved him. And it had turned out that Katerina had been exactly right, although she knew that Marcos had loved Alyssa and had been devastated by her death. But as a mother, his mother and as only a mother knows her children, she had never believed Alyssa was the love of his life, but she hoped that when the right woman came along, he would then know the difference, even if it was a hard lesson to learn.

Katerina had arrived as soon as the news of Dante's kidnapping had reached her, but now with Nikos in jail awaiting trial and Lucy feeling hurt and abandoned by Marcos, she'd announced she was going home.
Like Eleanor, she too thought he was a fool and needed to sort himself out. So, she had decided she was going home and letting him do just that. He'd tried asking her to stay a few more days while he attempted to find someone else or sort something out, but she'd merely said *no* and reminded him that if he could work out multi-million-pound deals, then he could work out what everyone else already knew. She wished

him luck, told him she loved him and to hurry up and get on with it.

And so now, in the quietness of his office, he sat and thought – thought about his son, his late wife, his business, what his life had been like, what he had and what he wanted.

He thought about his marriage to Alyssa, the partying, the glamour, the realisation now that it had been more like being part of a show, not a normal relationship where couples meet in the kitchen and actually talked whilst having a glass of wine and cooking, sharing their day's events even if it was a quiet day when nothing much had really happened, just enjoying each other's company. And even though he and Lucy weren't exactly a couple, that was what he had looked forward to every night and thought about at random times throughout his day. And suddenly, there it was. The realisation that he was in love with her. Maybe this was another reason it was all hurting so much. Only the other day he'd been thinking about asking her if she would like a piano in the house, somewhere she could teach private lessons in the hours she spent alone whilst Dante was at nursery. All along in his mind, he'd been looking for ways to make her stay. He had known she had feelings for him; he'd seen it, sensed it in her body language when she was around him, yet neither had spoken a word about how they felt about each other. And now this, him blaming her meant she'd been let down twice now, firstly by an asshole like Nikos and now by himself, a stubborn, selfish fool. It really was time to sort himself and this mess out.

Somewhere in all this his mobile was ringing, interrupting his thoughts dragging him back to the moment. Glancing at his phone, Marcos saw it was the nursery. Why would they be phoning him unless something was drastically wrong? Quickly he grabbed it, panic rising up inside him, its impact feeling like a massive wave about to hit the shore.

"Marcos speaking," he answered.

"Mr Petrakis?" the voice on the phone asked.

"Yes, speaking."

"This is Martha at the nursery, please don't be alarmed but over the last hour Dante has started to become unwell.

We've been monitoring his temperature but it's continuing to rise, and a rash has now started to appear. We are becoming concerned and would like you to come to the nursery straight away please, sir."

Marcos literally leapt from behind his desk, grabbing his suit jacket, keys and phone. He raced through the office door, calling out to Eleanor as he did so, "Please call my mother at the house. Dante has taken ill."

The traffic was heavy and by the time Marcos made it to the nursery, he was out of his mind with worry. He'd telephoned them from the car whilst on his way, but all Martha could say was that Dante was the same as when they had last spoken, and they were glad he was on his way.

Once inside the nursery, Marcos quickly spoke to Martha, who explained Dante had seemed to start the day a little out of sorts, but there had been nothing they could specifically put their finger on. They thought maybe he was tired or starting with a cold, or even missing the fact it hadn't been Lucy who had dropped him off. But in the last hour or so, he had become quite unwell, giving them cause for concern.

Bundling the hot, sweaty, quiet, listless Dante into the car, Marcos felt his fear growing with every passing minute, never in his life had he felt this scared and alone.

The nursery assured him they would ring the hospital ahead of his arrival, so they were in the picture. The traffic was steady, but the journey still seemed endless. Luckily when they did finally get there, there was a car parking space right near to the emergency entrance. Gathering Dante into his arms, Marcos rushed inside towards the desk, where even before he spoke, a nurse said his name and asked him to follow her straight away. Once inside a side room, a doctor appeared and immediately started asking lots of questions. He wanted to know Dante's name, age, symptoms and how long he'd been unwell and although it was all relevant, it all took time, and suddenly there it was again, that scared and lonely feeling, and he knew he needed Lucy there with him. The doctor told him within minutes Dante needed to be admitted and he would be transferred as soon as possible to the baby ward, where he would put into isolation while they conducted tests for meningitis. Next, the doctor was asking about Dante's mother and Marcos had to explain that she had passed away. The doctor apologised for all the questions but said they were all necessary in cases were the illness was possibly very serious, and both parents needed to be informed. But the next question he asked completely floored Marcos.

"While we're waiting for any previous notes to come over, and of course we would check anyway, but do you know Dante's blood group?"

Marcos felt his heart sink. The time had finally come for the truth to come out, and it couldn't have come at a worse time. Already filled with fear, now he needed to tell them what Alyssa had said to him that night. Finally he was going to learn the truth, whether this beautiful little boy, who he loved unconditionally and with all his heart, was really his.

Lucy couldn't stop pacing the room. Her mum had phoned to tell her the news that Dante had taken ill. Marcos was at the hospital now along with Katerina, who luckily had not yet left for home. All Lucy could think was that she wanted to go to them or at least phone Marcos, but what would she say?

She could text but then perhaps have to wait forever for a reply, not knowing if he was too busy or simply ignoring her and how was she going to feel then! Minutes felt like hours, and yet who was she to them anyway – why should he even bother to reply? She felt there was nothing she could do. Just when she thought she had the tears under control here they were again running uncontrollably down her cheeks. Would this ever end?

Suddenly, her phone buzzed, she grabbed it, desperate to see what the message said. Her mum had promised she would pass on any updates she received from Marcos or Katerina, straight away. *Poor Mum!* She felt Lucy at least deserved to be kept informed of how Dante was doing. But it wasn't her mum. It was Marcos.

'Lucy, I need you with me here at the hospital. Marcos X.'

The time it took her to grab her bag, keys and rush out to her old clapped-out car, was about as much time as it took her to reply: *'OK, I'm on my way, X.'*

Not sure she obeyed the speed limit, not really sure what route she had taken, she only knew somehow she had arrived and was dashing down the hospital corridors to the ward, her heart racing for more reasons than she could possibly comprehend.

What's happening?

Why did he want her here?

How sick was Dante?

Had he forgiven her?

Now reaching the ward she buzzed and waited for someone to allow her to enter. Her heart was beating so loud and fast that she was sure it sounded like she had a bomb strapped to her chest. And although she was stood outside the closed door waiting for it to be opened, she couldn't stand still, hoping from one foot to the other, desperate to get to the other side. A nurse appeared and asked who she was, and who she was here to see, then quickly pointed her in the direction of a side room.

Gently knocking, Lucy opened the door. But as she peered inside, there was nobody there. She looked back quickly, but the nurse was already half way down the corridor.

It seemed she was just left there to wait. And there wasn't even any evidence that Marcos and his mother had actually been inside of the room, but the nurse seemed sure this was where she would find them, so she stepped inside and took a seat.

Only minutes later, the nurse reappeared, "Lucy?"

"Yes," she replied. "Mr Petrakis and his mother are with Dante. The doctor is also with them now. If you would like to come with me, you should join them. Mr Petrakis is expecting you."

"Is Dante OK?" she asked, a lump forming in her throat, tears welling up in her eyes. Unable to disclose anything but obviously feeling her concern, the nurse simply said, "I'm sure all will be explained to you when you join them but don't worry. It appears to be a virus and a heat rash, but I'm sure Mr Petrakis will tell you more, and it seems all the blood tests have been in his favour."

Lucy couldn't help wondering if she meant Marcos had actually asked for or had needed to have the DNA test done. It did sound like that was what she was implying, but it was obviously not her place to say.

Thanking the nurse, Lucy stood outside the room where Marcos, his mother and Dante were gathered. The walls of the room were mainly glass and a large percent, though not all, were opaque so she could easily see what was going on inside. The three of them all huddled together, hugging. Dante in Marcos' arms, the little boy hugging his father, arms tight around his neck, whilst Marcos also had an arm around his mother, and she in turn, hugged them both close to her. It wasn't a moment she felt she could interrupt, nor a moment she felt she could be included in. They were all family and had each other, and she was not. And with tears streaming down her face, Lucy turned and walked away.

She sat in her old but faithful car in the car park, quietly gathering herself together. She knew now they would be fine. It looked like the traumas of today had been worthwhile, and whilst it must have been at times one of the scariest moments of Marcos' life, at least now, with no real harm done, they would finally be able to move on as a real family with no fear of tomorrow.

Finally having got herself together, she started the car and drove back to her mum and Steffos' house. She knew now it was time to sort her head out and make plans for the future – her future. It may be a long road ahead but she was strong and at times wilful, she knew it was time to get back on her own two feet and face life's challenges.

She hadn't wanted anything to eat that night and couldn't quite catch her sleep. And so, by morning she felt like she had a hangover even though she'd hadn't had any alcohol. She felt lousy and wondered if maybe now after all that had happened, she was going down with something, maybe a cold, but felt sure she'd be fine again in a few days.

During the days that followed being back home, Lucy received two e-mails offering her interviews for jobs she'd recently applied for. So now it seemed the ball was rolling for her and maybe it was time to start looking forward. The first was in a music school offering privately paid tuition, teaching both adults and children. The other was in a local high school teaching art. Both were very different, both within her capabilities and qualifications, so maybe the best thing was to try for both. She just needed, between now and the weekend, to get her possessions back from the big house, not a task she was at all looking forward to.

Marcos had felt exhausted when they'd all arrived back from the hospital. Katerina had agreed to stay on a few more days under the circumstances, which had been a great relief to him. Dante had been given antibiotics after being diagnosed with an ear infection, and cream for the prickly heat caused by his high temperature. The DNA had proved Dante was 100% his son and he knew now on reflection that he should never have doubted it. Alyssa was young, still desperate to have fun and go partying, and maybe had even struggled with post-natal depression. He'd been busy and blind to her struggles, but Dante's arrival had filled his life with unquestionable love and given him a different outlook. It had made him want to strive even higher and build up his empire greater still for his precious young son. But for Alyssa, motherhood had clearly filled her life with dread. Dante hadn't been planned and although he knew she had always loved him, he also knew that he hadn't fit into her world, their life or the life she had envisioned for herself or for them. So she had fought it all the way, blamed him, caused arguments, thrown tantrums and even thrown that dreadful accusation in his face on that fateful night, making him feel he'd been a totally inadequate and inattentive husband. But the picture was much clearer now. They just simply hadn't wanted the same lifestyle. Their marriage had been full of lust, not love. There was no denying their nights of passion, but had they ever made love? He had made love that night with Lucy. Lucy made him want to chat in the kitchen, feed ducks in the park, talk about the day, share a meal and even to cook for her. Lucy made him want to come home. Alyssa had never made him feel like that. He knew, at times, he'd simply stayed late at work because it was easier than listening to her want to get a babysitter and go out yet again. She'd wanted to employ a nanny because it was tiresome looking after a baby and inconvenient taking him when she wanted to have her hair or nails done. Yes, in her own way, she had loved him, but he was sure it would have been enough for her to kiss him good morning and good night.

Yes, everything seemed so much clearer to Marcos now, except why Lucy had not stayed at the hospital. Had she changed her mind and decided it was for the best to put it all behind her?

He had decided not to contact her that night, emotions were running high and a good night's sleep would be a better way to approach a new day. But he hadn't slept well. No, he'd slept like a man with a troubled mind. He knew now what he wanted, but he wasn't sure how to go about getting it, and the thought of rejection from the woman he loved was already filling him with fear.

It was Thursday morning and knowing that her first interview was on Tuesday, Lucy knew she needed to make the call to arrange a convenient time to go and collect her possessions. But she also knew she wasn't ready yet to hear the sound of his voice, or to answer any unexpected questions he may throw at her. So, she simply sent a text. At least in a text, he wouldn't hear her voice tremble at the sound of his, neither would she break down and end up sobbing because she didn't really want to take her things back out of the house. Because really, she wanted it all to be like it was before.

'Hi, Marcos. Hope you are all well. Really could do with collecting my stuff as soon as possible please, as I have job interviews early next week.

Lucy X.'

'Hi, Lucy. Yes, I quite understand. Could you come to the house on Saturday evening about 7:00 pm. I'd prefer Dante to have gone to bed before you arrive, so he's not upset.

Marcos X.'

The message brought her to tears again. Now, he didn't even want her to have a last minute with Dante. The sooner she got this all behind her the better, because right now, she didn't feel like she was ever going to be able to stop crying.

And so, it finally came. How can one day be so long? Most Saturdays are days off and one of the fastest days of the week, but this one had been everlasting. She was finally ready to go but why she'd bothered to make an effort with her appearance was beyond her.

She told herself it was for her own confidence, to make herself feel better, help her handle the situation. But her heart said: *Who are you kidding? You're crazy about him. You've checked yourself from head to toe at least fifty times and had a 2-hour clothes' crisis at the very least. I just hope he appreciates it, or lady, you are going to be there again, crying.* From the outside, she thought she looked calm and casual, make-up on but not too heavy, hair loosely blow-dried. Sleeveless navy linen shirtdress falling to just above the knee, mid-height tan leather wedges and just in case it turned cool, an off-white cardigan with large mint and blue flowers patterned on it. At that she did have to ask herself, how long do you think you are staying? Then a quick spray of her favourite perfume and she was ready. It was Lancome's *La Vie Est Belle* – Life is beautiful. And she hoped one day it would be again. Finally she added just a little more coral lip gloss that seemed to always bring the colour of her eyes to life, but she couldn't unfortunately do anything about the butterflies in her stomach, her sweating hands and her pounding heart. But from the outside she thought she looked alright.

She didn't remember the drive there, she just seemed to arrive at the large gates.

No longer an employee, no longer anything to any of them, she was just one more visitor who waited to be allowed entrance she no longer had a remote control to open the gates. She was about to lean out of her car and buzz the control, but Marcos must have been watching because before she was able to, the gates began to open. This was it, Lucy thought, the moment of goodbye was about to begin. She drove slowly down the long driveway to the house, pulling up outside and nervously getting out of her car, the anxious uncertain feeling rising and falling in her stomach whilst her heart raced and beat like a drum. The front door opened, and Marcos stood on the doorstep, his tan chinos and white linen shirt making him look more handsome than ever and making her feel more insecure than she'd ever felt in her life.

"Please, come inside," she heard him say as she walked towards the door. And without replying, she simply stepped inside.

"Would you like a coffee?" he asked, leading the way towards the kitchen.

"I'm fine," she replied. "I wouldn't like to interrupt your evening."

"I'll put the coffee maker on then, because you're not interrupting my evening." And with that there seemed no option other than to follow him into the kitchen, although she couldn't understand why he wanted to drag this out. Maybe it wasn't emotionally painful for him, maybe he saw it as the end of a business formality.

Marcos poured two coffees then sat down at the breakfast bar, whilst Lucy remained standing feeling like a mouse cornered by a cat, his eyes watching her.

At last, the silence was broken as he asked her,

"So, Lucy, how have you been?"

"Fine," she said. Because what else could she say? *(Oh! I've cried day and night, missed you both like crazy and can't believe you actually left me to the police, thinking so little of me!)* "Yes, fine."

"I'm sorry, Lucy," he was saying now, "for not trusting in you. For letting you down. I was just so upset and shocked when it turned out to be your ex-boyfriend. My mind just ran riot. When I had time to reflect, I knew you could never do a thing like that. The way you have been with Dante is as beautiful as any real mother could be with her child, and I'm sorry, Lucy, that it's come to this."

"It's all right, Marcos," she could hear herself saying. "I would have probably reacted the same, and we both know this was only a temporary arrangement. We just didn't quite anticipate how it would end."

"Here's a cheque for your sudden loss of income and the keys to the Mercedes you were driving. It's yours," he continued.

Lucy was furious! And for a moment speechless, "So just let me just recap what you're saying, Marcos. You're giving me a cheque, for, oh let's see, €10,000 euros for sudden loss of earnings and a posh car to swan around in so you can sleep in your bed at night and not have to feel like a guilty asshole. Well screw you, Marcos. When I came here, you needed a favour and I needed a job. I cared, I still care about Dante and have done from literally five minutes after I was introduced to him. Spending time with him meant it wasn't about money anymore. And if you think you can make yourself feel better for getting it so wrong and try to pay me off to relieve your guilt, you can go to hell, or anywhere you like, as long as I don't have to lay eyes on you again. Now, if you'll excuse me, I'll get my stuff together and get out of here."

"Lucy… wait, please. I didn't mean it like that. I was just trying to say I'm sorry. Without you, I'd be missing out on so much in my life. When I was with Alyssa, nothing was enough. I thought it was a normal relationship, but it wasn't if I wasn't giving her gifts or we weren't attending parties. She wasn't happy. And I'm not saying there haven't been other women since then – there have. But they've also been women who just wanted power and money and lifestyle. And then Lucy, there was you. You, who made life simple, kept it simple and made me see the little things that were important."

"I'm glad, Marcos, that you've learnt to appreciate the little things, so don't feel you need to treat me like your other women, at least I did something right," she replied.

"None of us are ever too old to learn something new from somebody else. Your mum told my mum about the DNA test, and there is no doubt that Dante is yours. You must all feel so totally relieved. I've had to laugh though, our mums have become quite bosom buddies from what I hear when they are on the phone, Women are never too old for girly chats, so out of this whole crazy scenario, there have at least been some plusses."

Lucy turned now and headed to what had for the last couple of months been her bedroom. She didn't want the chat to break down her barriers, she didn't want to end up crying and emotional. She just needed to get on with it now, gather her things and go.

It felt strange to be standing back in what she thought of as 'her' room. The whole ambience of the house had started to feel like home and now once more, she was about to be starting all over again. This time, she would take the time to find out what was truly right for her, a home she could call her own. Then, no matter what happened, it would still be hers. She dragged the suitcase from underneath the bed and put it on the top. She opened it up and told herself she needed to just get on with it.

But instead, she found herself sitting next to it with her head in her hands.

"Penny for them," Marcos said from the open doorway, where he was standing, watching her whist leaning against the doorframe.

"It's a blank canvas," she replied, "so you'd be wasting your money."

"No amount of money I would choose to spend on you, Lucy, would I ever consider to be wasted," he responded.

"This won't take me long, Marcos, so if you'll just give me a few minutes, please."

"You don't have to go, Lucy. I've said I'm sorry, and I got it wrong."

"Marcos, you've just tried to pay me off for your guilt, and we both know this was only a temporary arrangement. And I've already told you I don't want your money or your flash car. It's better for both of us to just leave it here, put it behind us and move on."

"But what if that's not what I want, Lucy?"

"Marcos, I don't know where you're going with this. Or what you hope to achieve and I'm not sure either I want to hear it. Because right at this moment, I definitely don't understand it."

"It's simple, Lucy. You pack and take your things out of the front door, or you just take your things into my room and make it our room."

She couldn't help but just stare at him. She thought she knew what she heard him just say, but truthfully, she needed a repeat to be sure. If she was wrong, she would be totally devastated and in a worse state than ever. Damn the man for making her feel like this!

Feeling her confusion, he repeated, "So which will it be, Lucy? The front door or our bedroom door?"

"And then what Marcos? Become your lover and childminder all in one, for as long as it suits you," she snapped back at him.

"Can't you see what I'm trying to tell you, Lucy?"

"No, Marcos. I can't see anything. So if you have something to say, just say it for God's sake because five minutes from now, I'll be gone, and it will be too late."

"I love you, Lucy. I want you to be my wife and my lover. I want you to be my best friend. Dante's mum, mother to more children if you'd like them, or if you wish, a career first or teach private lessons. I don't know, Lucy. I just know I love you and I want you to stay.

Suddenly the realisation of what he was saying registered in her mind and before she knew she was even about to do it, she was off the bed and throwing her arms around his neck. "I love you too, Marcos, so very much."

"So, does this mean you'll marry me?" he asked again.

"Yes, it does. And become Dante's mum, and I'd love to have more children with you. And now I've answered your questions just kiss me please."

Epilogue

It had been twelve months now since Lucy first pulled up at the big house and waited to be granted permission to enter. Part of her felt like it was yesterday, the other like forever ago. Life was good, and finally after years of learning both what she wanted to be in life and what she wanted from life, she had finally found it.

From the moment Marcos had told her he wanted her as his wife and not just his lover, there had been no going back. They had moved on as a family. And now, today was the day to put it in writing, to say it aloud, make it legal in the eyes of God and the law of the land, surrounded by the people they loved.

Dante, now a boisterous happy little toddler, was to be a pageboy. The bridesmaids were her young nieces. And the ceremony small and informal, with only family and friends present. Marcos had thought they should have a big wedding as it was her first, and in his words – the last for them both. But for Lucy, none of that had mattered.

All she wanted was to be his wife and best friend. They had come a long way in a short time, and it was now time for new beginnings. And so she stood there in their bedroom, with her wedding dress on. Ivory in colour, floor length with crossover shoestring straps, the fabric satin, soft and sexy, delicately dressed in crystal sequins around the bottom edge that caught the light. Her hair had been softly curled and clipped up at one side. Her jewellery was simple; long, dangly earrings with a diamond drop, a wedding day gift from Marcos and the beautiful bracelet that had been her gift from Dante on the night of the dinner dance. And of course, her stunning solitaire engagement ring, which for now was on her right hand, sparkling as the light in the room found it. She'd applied her own make up, wanting to keep it natural and simple and now as the final touch, still her favourite perfume: *La Vie est Belle*, for truly, life *was* beautiful.

A gentle tap on the door told her Steffos and Dante had arrived to escort her down to the garden, their garden, where the ceremony would be held. Food and drinks would be served there later and there would be music and dancing until late.

There were eighty guests in total and she could hear the laughter and chatter as they approached. Then the music started playing and the guests all fell silent as Steffos slowly walked her down the garden aisle whilst she held Dante's tiny hand in hers. Marcos standing, waiting, wearing a look of love so great she felt her heart miss a beat. There were to be no presents. There was nothing they needed only each other. They had requested donations be given to the local hospital instead, to help women with post-natal depression. And as she walked towards her husband-to-be with her beautiful bridesmaids now behind her, she knew as the distance between them disappeared, so too did everyone else as they looked only to each other. This was the moment she had waited for all her life.